ABANDONED AND ALONE

Debora Merheb

Abandoned and Alone
Copyright © 2017 by Debora Merheb
All rights reserved

First Edition

This is a work of fiction. Names, characters, organizations, places, events, and incidents are either products of the author's imagination or are used fictitiously.

All rights reserved. In accordance with the U.S. Copyright Act of 1976, the scanning, uploading, and electronic sharing of any part of this book without the permission of the publisher is unlawful piracy and theft of an author's intellectual property except in the case of brief quotations embodied in critical articles and reviews.

The scanning, uploading, and distribution of this book via the internet or any other means without the permission of the publisher is illegal and punishable by law. Please purchase only authorized editions, and do not participate in or encourage electronic piracy of copyrighted materials. Your support of the author's rights is appreciated.

CONTENTS

ONE	5
TWO	15
THREE	23
FOUR	27
FIVE	34
SIX	44
SEVEN	50
EIGHT	60
NINE	66
TEN	74
ELEVEN	88
TWELVE	96
THIRTEEN	101
FOURTEEN	108
FIFTEEN	112
SIXTEEN	123
SEVENTEEN	129
EIGHTEEN	134
NINETEEN	137
TWENTY	142
TWENTY-ONE	148
ACKNOWLEDGEMENTS	153
ABOUT THE AUTHOR	154

ONE

They were abandoning me. A hint of nervousness roiled in my guts, but I swallowed it down. Sure, they weren't my real parents, and sure they didn't treat me like a real daughter, but for the second time I truly felt unwanted. I watched from the kitchen window as Mom opened the car's passenger side door and got in. Dad slipped into the other seat and kissed her before he closed his door. Only Andrew hesitated, one foot in the car, and searched the front porch with his eyes. For me, I hoped.

They were leaving to the airport, going to Italy without me. They'd only be gone for two months—I didn't mind that. My adoptive parents had never treated me with kindness, so a few months without them would be my own less glorious holiday. Only Andrew, my brother, had ever been anything close to real family. What did get me angry, though, was having to stay with my cousin, Sara.

Let's just say we didn't get along; she was a girly girl, and I was not. That's not to say I was fat or skinny, in fact people always told me I looked beautiful, but I didn't care about all that—no dresses, no makeup, no fussing for me, thanks. Sara called me "boyish" and pranked me endlessly because she didn't like me. Once, on a camping trip next to a river, she tipped my tent into the water. At night. The whole thing. And I was inside it. Let me tell you, I'm still plotting revenge on her for that.

"Ashley!" my brother called as he leaned against the car's back door. "Come say bye!" See? The only kind one. The only one who actually cared about me.

I walked out to the car and leaned into the passenger side window. "Bye Mom, bye Dad." I fake smiled. "I'll miss you guys," I lied.

"Yup, we'll miss you too." Mom said with a fake smile. My dad just ignored me and turned the radio on. You see what I mean? My face muscles ached with strain, but I kept that fake smile up until I had turned from the window. Then I smirked. They didn't go out of their way to hurt me, but they did not treat me kindly either. Sure, I was thankful they'd adopted me and all, but they'd never loved me in a tangible way. Wasn't that part of being adopted? Being loved? They bought me the bare necessities and smiled at me once in a while, but there were no hugs and cuddles and lavish gifts for me. In fact they ensured I knew I wasn't part of the family every chance they got. Like today; no loving family would leave their real daughter behind like this.

I wrapped my arms around my brother. "Bye Andrew," I said.

"Bye." He smiled, got in, and shut the door.

Sure, I was mad at him for leaving me, but in my seventeen years, he was the only one who'd ever loved me. Come to think of it, that's why I was angry. He was my best friend, I told him everything. He, at least, should have stayed with me...but no! He chose Italy over me. What an awesome brother.

Maybe it wouldn't be so bad here though. My aunt and uncle's house was located in a beautiful town, surrounded by nature. There was a forest a few minutes from their house and there were many shops near-by. *Think positive,* I told myself.

I jumped a bit as the car screeched and sped down the driveway, all the positive thoughts leaving my mind, I just sighed and turned my back on it—on them.

A high pitched scream rang down the hallway barely an hour into my stay at Aunt Suzy and Uncle Tom's place. I leapt from the chair and ran towards the screams. Aunt Suzy and Uncle Tom cut in front of me in the passage and I nearly slammed into their backs. They looked as shocked as me. We ran together, following the screams which led to the kitchen where we found—you guessed it—Sara.

"What?" we screamed collectively.

"A- a- a-" She pointed at the kitchen table. "A s- s- spider!"

Sure enough, there on the table sat a spider the size of my finger nail, black as night and wriggling its round bottom, but it had no fangs, and its forelegs weren't lifted in an attack of any kind. It seemed oblivious to us. "You are so weird," I said and scowled at her as I picked up the spider and let it out through the window.

"Eww!" She shook her hands and squealed. "I can't believe you touched that disgusting thing."

"No need to be such a drama queen. You realize that you're fifteen and not four, right?" I asked her.

"Who do you think you are? First you come into my house, ruining what was supposed to be *my* vacation, and then you *insult* me. You're so pathetic."

I balled my fists and bit down my anger. I was being pathetic? Honestly, being called a four year old wasn't even an insult, so she was the one being pathetic. She was way too over-dramatic for her own good.

"Oh, well that really cut me deep. When you come up with better insults, call me." I said as I walked away from her.

"No wonder your real parents abandoned you," she growled, her blue eyes like ice. "And now your adoptive parents also want to get rid of you, so *I'm* stuck with you."

Her words stung, but I swallowed the sadness and the ache in my chest and balled my fists. This wasn't the first time my adoption had been thrown in my face. I found myself lifting my fist and punching her square in the jaw before I'd registered the action. It hurt my knuckles but it buried the pain. My auburn hair hung over my eyes, and I huffed like some thug. It felt good.

Tears wet her cheeks and she held her jaw, frowning at me. I could see she wanted to reciprocate, her mouth hung open, and I swiped the hair out of my eyes, silently daring her to try it.

"That's enough," her parents said at the same time. Aunt Suzy tugged me away by the arm, and I gave in. If this continued something bad might happen. Besides, I had won this bout, better to quit while you're ahead, right?

"Both of you go to your rooms now," Aunt Suzy said. Her voice was calm. I shrugged and smiled at Sara from behind Aunt Suzy.

"And Sara," Uncle Tom said pointing at her. "What you said was unacceptable." He put his hands on his hips and Sara pushed out her lower lip. "You're grounded for a month," he said. "Now go to your room."

I smirked at her again and waved before climbing the stairs. From the kitchen I heard her protest, and I smiled smugly. When I got to my room I slammed the door and fell face-first on my bed. We'd already fought, and I'd only been here for one hour. How would I survive two whole months?

One day had passed and I had survived, mostly by distracting myself with unpacking my things into the white closet against the wall of my room and thinking of the things that I could do to Sara as revenge for what she had said to me. Although I had already punched her, her words still hurt and I wanted to come up with some good revenge. What were the things that would annoy her? I folded a shirt and pulled out another, barely aware of my fumbling through the bag. I imagined sneaking into her room and stealing her makeup, or her beloved high heels. Or ripping all her oh-so-fashionable dresses, or putting bugs in her food. I imagined a bowl of pasta flying, her toppling from her chair and screaming. Or I could sneak into her room while she slept and draw a mustache on her face with a permanent marker. The idea of her prissy face with a large mustache drawn on gave me giggles. That was a good one. And then, of course, I could put a fake spider in her bed. I imagined her freaking out when she woke up with a spider next to her. Maybe she'd fall out of the bed. Ha! I really liked that option.

Yes, I'd go to the shop next door as soon as possible and buy a fake spider and permanent marker. In your face Sara! She'd learn not to mess with Ashley Nadia Jones.

After unpacking and tacking up my few posters, I got ready to go out. The day wasn't too cold, but I threw on a red hoodie anyway and tucked loose strands of my hair inside it. Then I grabbed my wallet from the counter and stuffed it into a pocket. Right, I was ready. I opened the door and walked to the stairs.

"Where do you think you're going, huh?" Sara stood right behind me, and I clutched the balustrade with one hand. Her jaw looked blue and swollen, and I bit my lips to keep from laughing.

"None of your business." I cocked my head and smiled halfway. "Oh, by the way, I like what you did to your face, is it a new makeup style or something?" Before she could relent, I walked down the stairs.

"You brat, you ruined my face."

"Well actually, it was already ruined, I just added some spice to it."

"You are going to pay for this."

Oh no Sara, you are. "Oh, is Miss Diva threatening me?" I covered my mouth, feigning shock.

"Yes, I am," she hissed, "so you better watch your back."

"You better watch your back," I mocked in a high pitched voice.

With one last threatening look, she stomped back to her room.

When I arrived at the store, I searched for a fake spider. The store sold many things, but not fake spiders: Makeup, cream, apples, juice, cigarettes...ah, I found a permanent marker, but still no fake spider. I searched the entire store without success and bought the marker with a sigh and a quick exchange of coins. Hopefully the next store had a fake spider.

The bell on the next store's door jingled as I walked in. From behind me came a scuffling noise. I spun around, but there was no one, so I assumed I had imagined it. This store had a fake spider, a big hairy one sitting on the first shelf. My smile grew to sinister proportions. Sara would regret saying what she had. And they had chocolate too. A sudden craving hit me, and I threw in two Hershey bars with my spidey purchase.

"Pff." A laugh threatened to burst from my lips but I stifled it with my fingers, the marker stuffed in my hoodie's pocket. A big, messy mustache spread out across Sara's face—yes, I'd drawn it, and I'd put the huge spider right next to her face too, balanced on the edge of the pillow so that it looked like it was just crawling over the edge, straight towards her face. This was going to be good.

The camera rested between a pencil case and a jar of coins on the desk nearest to her bed, giving me the ideal angle for the action about to transpire. That's right, I planned to post it on YouTube. Why prank without milking it for hits? I was trying to estimate just how many hits I would get when Sara mumbled in her sleep. The fun was about to begin.

"Harry," she mumbled into her pillow. Her head jerked up, then she lay her cheek back on the pillow. "Marry me, Harry Styles."

Hadn't she seen my spider? Realization dawned on me slowly—she talked in her sleep. How hilarious! I'd get at least ten thousand hits with this.

"Harry, sing to me!" She swatted at the air with one hand.

"Ha ha," I laughed but quickly covered my mouth. I didn't want her to wake up just yet. I had heard that if you talked to someone who sleep-talks while they were asleep, they'd sometimes answer, so I tried it. "What song do you want him to sing?" I snickered.

"OH, OH, OH, THAT'S WHAT MAKES YOU BEAUTIFUL!" She belted in her sleep.

I almost fell to the floor laughing. Big mistake, Sara shuffled in the sheets and rubbed at her eyes, and I knew she was going to wake up any second. As quick as I could, I shot into the cupboard and pulled the door almost shut.

"Ah!"

That was Sara screaming. Yup, she'd seen the spider. Sara was going to kill me for this, but I was having too much fun to care.

With a leap, Sara shot out of the bed, her blonde hair in a tangled mess. Her scream rose in pitch as she chucked a pink high heel at the fake spider, then a stick of mascara and lipstick, then a dirty sock and a bottle of hairspray. Nothing hit the spider, which was great for my video. When she realized the spider wasn't moving, her screaming abated. Man, was I happy her parents had left for a business meeting, because I would have been in big trouble with them.

Both hands covered my mouth, and I tried in vain to silence the guffaws rolling in my belly.

Sara stopped screaming altogether and approached the spider with caution, one toe at a time, as if it were a bomb. With a pen, she jabbed at it, cringed, and when she saw it wasn't moving, poked it with her finger. Of course it didn't move. The look on her face was worth all the effort.

"Ashley!" she screamed, so loud my ears hurt.

"Yes?" Coming out from inside the closet, I let loose the laugh I'd held in. With tears in my eyes, I grabbed my stomach, bent at the waist with the laughter. The mustache looked great on her face.

"This is not funny!" she shouted. Her nostrils flared, her fists balled, and she tried to punch me, but I stepped out of the way.

"Nice face," I stammered between laughs.

The confusion on her face turned to terror. She grabbed the mirror from inside her drawer, and her face went slack with horror when she saw my artwork.

"You are going to pay for this!" she squealed as she rushed at me with her fists clenched again. I rolled on the floor, laughing my butt off. She was furious, I promise I saw smoke rolling from her nostrils and ears.

Again she tried to jump on me, but I rolled away and grabbed the camera, focusing it on her fuming face while I retreated and ran for my room. She was close behind me, but I managed to lock the door before she got to it. She pounded on it and screamed, but it sounded like the war drums of victory to me. I plugged the camera into the laptop, humming, and put the video on YouTube.

Even though it had been a lot of fun destroying her face and her reputation online, I knew she would reciprocate, and the thought spoiled my great mood.

If only I'd known how devastating the consequences would be.

TWO

A heart locket lay in my palm and I opened and closed it over and over, looking at the picture inside. On one side of the heart was a picture of my biological parents and the other side was empty. My mother—golden hair and dark green eyes, the prettiest face I had ever seen. In the picture she looked strong and brave. I don't know why, she just did.

On the other side of my mom was my father—blue eyes, black hair, and as handsome as my mother was fair. He had an arm around my mom and he was smiling at her in admiration. As I stared at them both, I couldn't help but wonder why they had abandoned me, why they'd left me with nothing but the ache in my chest and the locket. What had I done to them to make them leave me alone in an orphanage, and at only four months old? Had I done something terrible? Had they been going through tough times? Had they lost their jobs? Had too little money to provide food for me? Or…or did they hate me?

So many questions that would never be answered. Deep inside me a hollow anger festered. Why would they leave me with a picture of them, why torture me with what I had lost? Sure, I was glad that I had a picture; at least I knew what they looked like, but I still wondered, *why?* Sighing, I closed the locket for the last time and dropped it on my bed.

As I walked down the stairs my stomach rumbled. I could smell eggs, and sure enough on the table were eggs and bacon. Yum! Only Aunt Suzy sat at the table; I don't know what I would have done if

Sara had been here. Aunt Suzy looked pretty tired, probably because of the business meeting.

"Hello dear," Aunt Suzy said with a warm smile, "how about some breakfast?"

"Hello to you too," I answered. "Sure. I would love breakfast. How was the business trip? How come you guys are back so early? I thought the place was, like, four hours away."

Aunt Suzy looked at me with tired eyes, "Well, you know your uncle, he doesn't like to leave Sara home alone, even worse; both of you guys. Also we both felt bad that we had to leave on the first night of your stay with us, so we left as early as we possibly could."

After Aunt Suzy said that, she turned away and grabbed the bowl of eggs, placing some in my plate. I smiled and dug in, but at the first taste my stomach did flip flops and I barely held it together. I usually loved eggs but it seemed as if Aunt Suzy had put sugar on the eggs instead of salt. The smell of the eggs had gone from deliciously scrumptious to a nauseating stench. Yuck.

"So..." I started, pushed my plate aside nonchalantly. "Where is my dear cousin Sara?"

"I haven't seen Sara this morning, actually," Aunt Suzy said between bites.

"Oh," I mumbled and shrugged, moving the eggs around on my plate and willing myself to take a bite. I just couldn't. We finished the breakfast in near silence. I say finish, but I really just mixed the eggs around on the plate until Aunt Suzy had finished. "Thank you, that was delicious."

Aunt Suzy smiled and nodded, her eyes flitting to my still full plate and back at my face.

"Aunt Suzy," I said, "I'm feeling a bit off. I think I'm going to go out for a walk, get a bit of fresh air. I'll be back in a bit."

She stood and gathered the plates, mine on top because it was still full. "Alright, dear."

Outside the air was crisp and fresh. I had decided that I would go to the park. Already the fresh air had taken away some of that queasiness, and now I only wished for something to take away the awful egg taste lingering on my tongue.

As I neared the park I heard another scuffling sound behind me similar to the sound I'd heard the day before, and I spun on my heels determined to catch whoever it was. A boy ran up the road in the other direction, but I hadn't seen his face and he was too far to try and catch. Who was he? Was he the one who had made the noise yesterday at the store? If he was, why was he following me? I shuddered. Was he following me or was I just imagining things? I was probably overreacting. He was just a guy going on a nice morning jog.

I turned around and made my way to the park with my hands in my pockets. The egg taste was fading, and I decided to just continue walking, willing myself to forget about my stalker. *Just a guy running*, I reminded myself. Yeah, that was probably what it was.

The park was great—it calmed me. The birds chirped at each

other, the trees danced in the wind. I must have spent a few hours there, strolling and enjoying the peaceful atmosphere. Sitting on the bench and humming to myself. Counting the ants trailing the pavement.

When I got back to my aunt and uncle's house it was past noon and I was smiling. I had missed lunch, and my stomach didn't like that, but at least I felt better. I kicked off my shoes, grabbed an apple from the display bowl in the kitchen, went up to my room, and opened the door.

There, standing near my bed, was Sara, swinging my locket on her finger with a smug expression on her face. My breath caught. Oh no.

My fingers suddenly felt numb, and I stood frozen in my place while Sara swung the locket, round and round. With each swing my heart twisted more, and the thumping in my chest grew louder. The apple fell, a hollow thud on the carpet. If she did anything to my locket, I didn't know what I would do. I know, it was just a locket, but this was the only thing I owned that mattered—the only piece of my real family and my mysterious past.

"Sara," I started. My voice shook even though I tried to keep control of it. I tried to smile but it must have looked more like a grimace. "Please give me my locket back." My voice had gone soft.

She pouted and batted her eyelashes, the locket swishing through the air. "And why, my dear cousin, would I do that?"

"Look," I growled and clenched my fists. I needed to calm down, but it was hard to do when she grinned that evil grin, holding my locket. "Just please give it to me. I don't want to cause problems."

"No, you look," she hissed. "Don't say I didn't warn you. Do you know how long it took me to get that mustache off my face?" When I looked closer, I saw her skin had been scrubbed raw and looked reddish.

My eyes widened, and I tried to swallow the panic, but my hands started shaking anyway. "I'm sorry okay, I was angr-"

"Sorry won't do it this time!" The locket stopped swinging, and she caught it with one angry fist.

How could she get angry about something as trivial as drawing a mustache on her face and putting a fake spider on her bed? She'd done much worse to me before. The injustice of it all turned my fear to anger.

"Give it to me now!" I shouted, "It's mine, not yours!"

Too late I realized that's what she'd wanted—she'd wanted to make me angry, she'd wanted to see me desperate. And I was desperate.

"Awe," she said in a condescending voice, "am I making you upset?"

I tried another tactic. "You will not do anything to my locket," I commanded and planted my feet on the ground.

"Oh yeah?" her eyes twinkled with mischief. "Well, watch me."

In less than a second, she'd shoved me aside and sprinted down the steps. Her shoes thump-thumped on the carpet, and I gave in to terror. As I chased her, I screamed. With a wildness in her eyes, she swung the front door open and leapt onto the pavement. I skidded as I rounded the corner and reached for the doorframe.

Even though I was a fast runner, I was barefoot so Sara was ahead of me by a few meters. My feet were hurting but I was finally catching up with Sara. Just as I thought that luck was on my side, Sara snaked through a crowd of people. Unfortunately for me, I bumped into a lady and fell to the ground. I apologized and quickly stood up, continuing the chase up the paved walkway, where I finally caught a glimpse of Sara running passed the shops, then turning left. I ran as fast as I could. I was sure I was gaining on her. She swerved right into another street, and my lungs started to burn. I pushed myself harder, intent on catching her before she destroyed my life. I had no idea where we were going, but deep inside I knew it was not good. Whatever she had planned for my locket was bad, and I had to catch her before she reached wherever she was headed. Though I wracked my brain for ideas, I came up with nothing. If she had wanted to crush my locket under a car or truck, she'd have thrown it out the window onto the street.

Maybe she wanted to sell it, but that wouldn't work with me chasing her down. By the time she stopped running all my muscles burned. Panting, I rested my hands on my knees.

We were in a grassy area surrounded by trees, except for the walkway on which I stood. In the middle of the expanse was a huge pond, which looked dark and deep.

Sara's chest heaved and sweat glistened on her forehead. "Say bye-bye to your precious locket!" she yelled with a manic expression.

Wait, what? The pieces clicked. "Don't you dare!"

It was too late. The locket left her fingers and arched through the air, taking my sanity and my heart with it. It hit the pond's surface and bubbled as it sank—the only memory of my parents. When I could no longer see it, I realized my mouth was hanging open. Tears formed in my eyes and an emptiness consumed me. The only memento of my parents gone, gone forever. Pain and hollowness consumed me. Tears drenched my cheeks.

When Sara saw me, something like guilt flashed in her eyes, but it vanished as fast as it had appeared. With one swing of her arm, she had broken my heart, and I'd make her pay.

Sara must have seen the look in my eyes because fear suddenly entered hers.

"I-I'm sorry." She practically whimpered.

I repeated her line. "Sorry won't do it this time."

I swung at her a few times but she dodged my fists.

Adrenaline pumped through my veins, but everything blurred with the tears in my eyes. My heart lay at the bottom of that pond and I was numb to my core. Sara and her stupid pranks. My adoptive parents who didn't care. My brother who betrayed me. My biological parents who had abandoned me.

Letting out a sob, I shoved Sara with all my strength and she yelped as she fell to the ground. My whole body tightened as I waited for her to stand up. After a moment, I wiped my eyes and cocked my head.

"Sara?" She didn't answer.

I knelt down next to her and gasped. The back of her head had hit a rock and there was blood flowing from a nasty looking cut.

Reality came into focus. I heard birds in the trees, leaves

shushing in the breeze, water lapping at the pond's edge. What had I done?

"Sara?"

She didn't move. A cold terror gripped me. What had I done! I felt fear running through my body. My heart was beating at an abnormal rate. All the anger inside of me turned into terror. I leapt up, turned, and ran. Away from Sara's limp body. Away from my locket and the pond. Away from my aunt and uncle's house. Away from everything.

THREE

    Blind with fear and rage, I ran and ran and ran. Time flew by, and my legs whizzed past things I didn't care to notice. It seemed my life had reached a critical point. Nobody loved me, and I thought I might have just killed a girl for a locket. My heart wrenched in my chest, but it was not for Sara, it was for one of the only thing that had mattered to me: my locket. Tears ran down my cheeks as I sprinted. My lungs started aching and I ignored them just as I ignored the burning in my muscles.

    Then all at once my knees buckled and I fell into the dirt, verdure and rotting forest gunk. Gross. I crawled to the nearest tree and leaned against its trunk while my breathing calmed. Light danced through leaves high above my head, but my traumatized brain couldn't grasp what it was. I glimpsed passing clouds and a blue sky as a light breeze rushed through the leaves. My heart calmed. Where was I? How would I get back to my aunt and uncle's house? Should I even go back, after what happened? I bit my lip.

    Unable to decide what to do next, I wandered aimlessly past trees, so many trees. This must be the forest. My feet ached, caked with muck. I hadn't had time to put on shoes and my feet were blistered and bleeding. My tongue clung to my pallet, and my lips felt cracked. A headache threatened at my temples.

    Then I heard a truly welcome sound: rushing water. A sip of water sounded like a slice of heaven right then. I rushed towards the sound till I reached a small waterfall, about the same height as me. Extending my hands, I let the cool water fall into my open palms, then stuck my face straight into it and drank as much as I could between breaths. The cold water on my face and hot neck was so refreshing, and it soothed the burn in my throat from that crazy run.

I looked at the natural pool of water gleaming below the waterfall, calling to me, and with one smooth movement, I stood and thrust myself into the water. As I hit icy water, my muscles relaxed and my skin was cooled. I broke the surface and sighed out the tension. The natural pool was pretty deep for such a small waterfall. It felt amazing. The waterfall was not that big and I knew that there were many small waterfalls in this wood. I had already been in these woods once and I had walked around for hours. I had found three different small waterfalls.

I spent a few hours swimming and drinking water, and finally pulled myself up onto the rocks to dry in the sun. One problem solved, I had water. The sun dried my clothing. My stomach was growling like a bear, ferocious and unrelenting. I'd have to go find food somewhere. The next challenge on my list: food.

I blatantly blocked out thoughts of Sara and my locket and everything to do with a painful life waiting for me out there. That was for another time.

The trees all around me were tall and since it was impossible to figure out where I was or where the closest food might be, I decided to climb a tree. I found a medium length one that was close to the water. Grabbing a branch, I tried to pull my body upwards. My body was still sore from the run and I wasn't able to heave it more than a few inches off the ground.

I sighed and closed my eyes. *Come on Ash, just like when you were a kid and you and Andrew climbed trees all the time.* With a grunt, I pulled with all the strength that I had left in my body. I smiled to myself as my feet touched the branch. The rest would be easy now; the branches were all close to each other.

When I reached the top, I spotted more trees, but I wasn't high enough to see past them.

As I was heading down, I caught a movement below and thought I saw two figures. My heart raced, but as fast as the figures had appeared, they disappeared. Was someone following me? I shook my head and tried to convince myself that it was just animals. Why would someone follow me?

Branch by branch, I made my way down, and added arm-ache to my list of troubles as I headed to a taller tree. Before I could reach the tree though, a strong arm wrapped around my waist and a hand covered my mouth. Fear jolted through my body, and I tried screaming, but the screams were muffled by the hand covering my mouth. I thrashed and struggled, but whoever held me was strong. The panic inside built.

"Stop moving," the voice said, and I was surprised that it didn't sound all raspy and creepy like those stalkers on Channel 177 who killed girls in the woods. "We're not going to hurt you, just calm down!" That's when I noticed that there was another guy in front of me. And he looked kind of familiar. Who did they think they were to hold me down like this? I bit the guy's hand and growled, "Who are you? What do you want with me?"

"I'm not going to do anything to you," the guy in front of me said, and the other one swore behind me, clutching his hand. "I'm

Joshua, your nephew." He smiled and stretched out his hand for a handshake. This guy was crazy, I had no nephews. My mind thought of escape routes, but it was impossible to figure out which way would lead to civilization. "We're taking you to your brother, your real, blood brother," he said, letting his hand drop.

"What?" I shouted. What he was saying hit me, and it felt like the air had been knocked from my chest. Was he telling the truth? Did I really have a brother? I suddenly felt dizzy, and my stomach felt like it was digesting itself with hunger. I gasped for air. It was impossible, wasn't it?

FOUR

At that moment everything froze, like water in the deep frost of winter. The guy behind me stepped back, still clutching his injured hand to his chest. My heart was chilled by Joshua's simple words and my throat felt constricted, like tiny hands were closing around my neck with a grip as strong as iron. My brain refused to register the information, it couldn't be true...

"That's not true," I said, voicing my chilling thoughts. His face crinkled with confusion as he studied my face. I felt all the color leak from my complexion. He seemed honest.

"I can prove it," he said. "Your mother's name was Sandra, and your father's was John. Your family's maiden name is Coffman." His voice never faltered and was strong with confidence. The names sparked recognition, but I refused to let it show on my pale face. Those were common names, I had probably just heard them at school or something. He couldn't be telling the truth.

"Lunatics!" I screamed at the top of my lungs, and turned to flee when Joshua caught my wrist with a feverish grip.

"You are not my nephew!" I spat.

"We're not lunatics." The deep voice caught my attention.

Joshua let go of my wrist, and I whipped my head around. Behind me stood a broad shouldered man, the man whose voice had shaken my guts. He stretched out his hand and closed my gaping mouth with a touch on the chin.

My heart skipped beats; I was being ambushed by people claiming to be long lost relatives in a forest where nobody would find my body.

"Look Ashley," Joshua said, "you need to c-"

"How do you know my name?" I yelled, "Have you been stalking me? Oh. My. Goodness. You're the guy who was following me, aren't you?"

"Please, calm down. I know who you are because you're my aunt. Kyle was the one trailing you." He shrugged and folded his arms. "He's been tracing your footsteps for some time now. He- I thought that since your adoptive parents had left you to go to Italy, maybe we could take you to your brother... my dad." It was too much to take in.

My hands trembled and darkness bled into my vision. A full-fledged headache set in as I thought of ways to question their competence. They'd made all this up to get me to come with them willingly to some abandoned shack where they could chain me up and torture me for weeks. But then, they could just have grabbed me and dragged me there. Why the lies? I took a few deep, shuddering breaths.

"Okay, prove it," I said, closing my eyes. "Prove that you're my nephew and that I have a biological brother."

They said nothing and I clenched my fists.

"Prove it!" I shouted and glared at them. So they were lying, I just couldn't find an angle to explain why.

A smile crept onto the younger one's face as he fished a small folded photo out of his faded jean pocket. He ambled cautiously over to me, placing the cold paper in the palm of my hand.

It was an old picture of a young couple staring back at me. In the women's arms was a baby girl in a thin white dress, and beside the man stood a tall boy. I knew them. Those were my parents' faces. Was that me in their arms?

I dropped to my knees on the forest floor, and tears once again blurred my vision. I touched the little baby with my finger, as if it could bring back more memories or the feel of a loving mother's arms around her daughter.

"The boy there is your brother," Joshua said. "He got married when he was twenty, which was... a little less than two years after you were put up for adoption, I think. His wife –my mom- gave birth to me less than a year into their marriage. I'm fifteen now. And you're seventeen." It was true. All of it. However impossible this seemed, it had to be true. My mind reeled, refusing to accept it, but deep down I knew. This was it. I had a family. A real, blood family.

I had stayed silent for a long time before finally accepting their words. Now they claimed to be taking me to see the brother I had never known of. It took a lot of coaxing before I took their words as the truth, but for some reason a feeling deep in my gut told me that what they said was true. That picture could have come out of a hole in the ground for all I knew, but my heart was pulled towards honesty from their mouths, and I trusted them despite my best judgment.

I had grown up with Andrew as my brother without the

knowledge of this other man, and I couldn't help but wonder what it would feel like to meet my biological brother. I was shocked when I found out that I had been adopted. I was seven when I overheard my parents talking about how, no matter how hard they tried, they could not love me as though I was actually theirs. I had walked into their room and they had turned to stare at me in shock and guilt.

I was utterly confused until my mother said, "Ashley, you're adopted." That day I had felt hatred run through every fiber of my being. I had hated my real parents for abandoning me, hated my adoptive parents for not loving me as their own.

I was still angry with Andrew for choosing Italy over me...but what did I expect from him? I guess blood really was thicker than water.

It felt strange to be with real family, ones related to me through genetics and not linked to me by a piece of paper.

"My feet are killing me," I whined as we continued our trip.

"We're almost there," Joshua responded. I felt like we had been walking for hours, but without a watch the only way I could tell was by the sun setting behind the trees.

"I have a question. Did you really have to be so dramatic about taking me? Couldn't you just come and talk to be normally?"

Joshua let out a nervous laugh, "Where's the fun in that?"

I knew he was lying. There was something that he wasn't telling me, and I would find out.

A few moments later the trees became sparser and we stepped into a clearing. My jaw dropped at the sight before me. A multi-story house stood towering before me. The building was built from rustic wood and the roof of beautifully crafted red brick. Next to the house a babbling brook flowed into the dense green forest. There was nothing extraordinary about the house, but maybe the fact that it was in a forest made everything more alluring; as though the scenery was from a dream, a fantasy.

"Welcome to your brother's house!" Joshua said with a genuine smile. I felt a home in the house's presence. Such beauty!

Joshua grabbed my wrist and pulled me up freshly stained wooden stairs, and as he dragged me up the rickety stairs a face entered my thoughts. Sara. I thought about how she might have been searching for me. I threw the image from my mind and cast the thought into oblivion. As of this moment she didn't matter. When I realized that Joshua was still holding my wrist I quickly yanked it out and looked at the floor. First, he stalks me, then, he thinks that I'll just be okay with a total stranger grabbing my hand? It wasn't rocket science; don't touch a stranger to whom you just admitted you had been stalking.

Joshua cleared his throat and scratched his neck. "Sorry…" He mumbled. I just nodded and Kyle opened the front door while he chuckling quietly.

As we walked into the beautifully decorated home a young girl holding a half eaten cookie ran past me followed by two other children.

"We are the cookie monsters!" the older girl yelled. "We will eat you! Rawr!" A boy ran besides her. Her blonde hair trailed behind her as she chased the tiny girl. The little girl let out an adorable squeal and attempted to run faster to protect her cookie. I glanced around and realized that we must be in a living room. A younger boy with auburn hair was sitting on a long dust-colored sofa playing on an Xbox. His fingers darted around the small machine as I imagined he commanded his avatar around. He glanced up as we walked through the door and his eyes widened a bit before he went back to his game. No wonder the house was so big. I had already counted four children, not including Kyle and Josh.

"How many kids are there here?" I asked, wondering why my "brother" had so many nose miners crawling around his house.

"Well, including Kyle and I, there are eight kids. There are also twins somewhere, but I don't know where they are. Dad always felt bad about what he did to you so he adopted a few kids." Joshua covered his mouth, his eyes wide, no doubt shocked at his own words.

"What he did to me? What did he do to me?" I asked, confused.

Joshua's eyes widened further as he contemplated ways of scooting around his mistake. "Um, never mind. Forget I said anything at all."

I wouldn't let him. "No. I want to know. I have the right if it has anything to do with me," I spat. The children in the room stopped to stare at me and my angry words. Joshua ignored my whines, turning away to avoid further questioning.

"Fine. Be that way. I'll find out eventually," I said coldly.

"That she will," I heard Kyle mutter.

"Follow me," Joshua commanded, stalking out of the room. I followed, looking around at everything. We entered a long hallway lined with gorgeous antique wallpaper and ancient chairs. After a long trek down a hallway that seemed to stretch into infinity, Joshua stopped at a large door with intricate designs carved into the oak wood.

"Are you ready?" Joshua started. "He doesn't know that we went to get you -we were supposed to get you tomorrow, but we wanted to surprise him..."

"He told you to get me?" I was a little scared, but the rest of his sentence sank in and panic started clawing at my resolve. I took a step back, but Kyle was behind me. "So that's it?" I frowned at Kyle, then at Joshua. "I just walk in there and say, 'Oh, hi, nice to meet you. I'm your sister by the way.'"

They looked at me as if it made the most sense and I growled and ground my teeth.

"I can't do that!"

"Calm down," Kyle said with a reassuring smile. "We'll go with you."

I rolled my eyes. "Wow, I feel so much better now that two strangers are coming with me to meet another stranger." I muttered under my breath.

Josh's hand wrapped around the silver door handle and turned it with a slight "click". My heart was racing in my ears and my hands began to shake. "Here goes nothing." I said. But this was not nothing; this was everything.

FIVE

The room had a massive fireplace built into one wall. The carpets were rich, embroidered maroon and cream patterns too intricate to follow. A large mahogany desk, impeccably kept, not a paper or pencil in sight, stood at the other end of the room, and a bookcase just behind it with equally neat and finely kept books that matched the room. And against a third wall was a large couch. Lounging on the couch with an elegant abstract throw over his legs was the man they said was my brother.

He had the same dark hair and light eyes as the man I had labeled "Father" in the folded photo that lay in my pocket. He looked exactly like them, like my parents. His box-shaped chin matched the square-ness of my father's face, and by the challenging gleam in his eyes I knew he must have my mother's bravery. Still I found it hard to believe. My whole life had been without them, without anybody truly connected to me. By blood. The idea seemed almost absurd. Too good to be true. But there he sat. Alive. Well. Totally normal.

I struggled to find words as he sat up and stared into my eyes with his ice blue ones and put aside the book he'd been reading. I had my mother's dark, moss green eyes and the same nose as my father, but besides that, I felt I had no resemblance to my blood family. Just thinking about this man sitting in front of me I was amazed. I never would have thought that I would meet anyone bearing relation to my parents. Never. It had never even crossed my mind that I might have siblings. I had always assumed I was an only child.

I stuck my hand out in a nervous spurt. "My name is Ashley...hi."

The man chuckled, his eyes crinkling at the edges.

"I know that, but you don't know me, do you? My name is Nathaniel, but everyone calls me Nate." He stood and met my eyes again with a big smile, then wrapped his warm hands around my clammy fingers and shook my hand gently.

Nate. Nate. Nate...I repeat his name in my head over and over again. This was too much for me to handle. Pent up emotions began to surface and stopping the tears was harder this time.

"I'm sorry," I started, tears welling in my eyes. "I just...I never knew I had a brother." I put my hand over my mouth to muffle a sob. Nate pulled me over and wrapped his strong, protecting arms around me in a warm hug. I embraced him back, hiding my face in his shoulder. He smelled strange, but I felt oddly at peace there. I trusted him, and I had no reason to besides his close resemblance to people I had never met. I pulled back as my emotions subsided and dried my face, feeling slightly embarrassed. I hated crying; it felt awkward.

I looked behind me and noticed that Kyle and Joshua had left the room.

"So, Ashley Coffman, huh?" I asked, pulling my sleeves over my hands and looking at the floor, blinking away the last moistness.

Nate chuckled. "Yeah, Ashley Coffman. My sister." I smiled at his welcoming words. "Would you like to meet my children?"

"Sure." I nodded and followed him out of the organized room, back into the packed living room where all the children had gathered. I trusted Nate and the gut feeling inside told me he could not be lying.

"I name is Wana," the little girl that had been chased earlier said in a cute baby voice.

Everyone was in the living room and the kids were introducing themselves to me one at a time.

"What she meant to say is that her name is Rana," the bigger girl said. "I'm Maya. She's two, I'm sixteen."

"We're Leah and Cynthia," two twin girls said at the same time, sitting together on the couch while braiding each other's hair. Wow...creepy. "We're thirteen."

"I'm Dylan and I'm fifteen," the boy that had been chasing Rana earlier said. "Dad, can I go now? I have things to do." He looked at Nate and Nate's jaw clenched, his arms folded over his chest. I just blinked a few times at Dylan. Wow… I had imagined that he would be friendlier by the way he'd been playing with Rana earlier.

"Dylan don't be rude!" Nate scolded.

"I'm not rude, I'm just asking if I can go."

"What do you have better to do? Play video games?"

"Um, yes." Dylan said it as if it was the most obvious thing in the world.

"Just go!" Nate said, looking really peeved.

Dylan stood up and left the room, hands tucked into his pockets, shoulders slumped.

"Sorry about him," Nate said looking at me and letting out a sigh.

"Hey! I didn't get to introduce myself," the boy who had been playing on the Xbox earlier said. "I'm Mark, I'm ten, and I'm the awesomerest one!" When he finished, he threw his hands out like an actor receiving applause on stage.

Maya scowled at him and folded her arms. "Awesomerest isn't even a word, dummy."

"I'm so awesome that I get to make up words!" Mark cried out.

Joshua had been leaning in the doorway, and he stood straighter and met my eyes. "You know who I am, but could you call me Josh? Just Josh, not Joshua. I prefer that."

"Sure," I nodded.

"Now you've met the crew. Maya could you please take Ashley to the guest room?" Nate's tone suggested that it was more of a command than a question. Maya nodded.

She stood up from the couch and tugged her shirt straight. I also stood up and followed her out of the living room.

"I'm happy you're here," Maya told me as we walked back down that long corridor.

"Um, thanks," I responded awkwardly.

"I really am; I mean, you are kind of my aunt. Dylan and I are adopted, so I guess you're not really my aunt but still, kind of."

My stomach growled and I tried hard to ignore it. "Yeah...." Wait what about Kyle? I mean he had to be adopted if he was my age. "What about Kyle, isn't he adopted too?" I asked, voicing my thoughts.

"Well no, Dylan and I were adopted when we were two and three. We're not siblings by the way, in case you were wondering. Kyle's parents died last year and my dad was his legal guardian, so technically he's not my brother or your nephew, but he lives here so…yeah he's like a brother."

I nodded taking in everything she said. That made sense.

Maya stopped in front of a room and opened the door. Inside was a big bed and a closet, a window looking out on the yard. The room was painted yellow, with light pastel curtains dancing in a slight breeze coming through the window, and the late afternoon sunlight bleeding onto the sheets and pillows.

"Well, this is your room for now," Maya said. "You can settle in and then I'll call you down for dinner when it's ready."

I nodded and Maya left me alone in the room. It seemed like a dream, such silky soft sheets on a massive, fluffy bed. So many pillows, all color coordinated, some with delicate flowers embroidered into the edges, others with yellow patterns. The last light dappled through trees and reflected off the water gushing outside, the soft breeze whispering through the curtains. My stomach growled again, but still I sighed in contentment. Could this be real? It seemed too good to be true.

"You didn't tell me we were having someone over," I heard a hushed voice say.

"Look, it's not just anyone," I heard Nate whisper. "Let me explain."

I was standing in front of the closed kitchen door, listening to my brother argue with someone. I had just finished settling in and had come to the kitchen, my stomach compelling me towards the enticing scents, when I started hearing sounds of an argument beyond the door and paused. Maybe I should have waited for Maya to come get me. It didn't seem like a good idea to head in and take a bite of whatever smelled so good anymore.

"Look Nathaniel, I don't care who it is! I already have ten people to feed. You expect me to make food for one more? We barely have enough for ourselves!" The new voice was decidedly feminine. Maybe Nate's wife?

I sighed. Clearly I was not wanted here. Of course I wasn't going to leave when I had only just found my brother after a lifetime without blood relatives. I would just go and find my own food. Easy. Whoever the woman was, she was right. Ten people to feed was enough, and I wasn't going to add to that. Especially not if it meant making my newfound family's lives harder than they already were. Curiosity filled me as I thought about something. How was it possible that people with such a big house and such fancy rooms had barely enough to eat? That seemed extremely weird.

I left the kitchen door without a touch and headed out the front door, making my way into the trees. Suddenly, I felt a light but firm tug on my shirt. I looked behind me and saw Rana -the youngest of my new nieces- looking at me with an open yet shy expression. I turned to face her and crouched so I could meet her eye-to-eye. "Hello Rana," I said, "do you need anything?"

"Can you pway wif me?" she asked in that adorable little voice, looking at me with big, expectant eyes.

"Of course I can play with you," I told her. "What do you want to play?"

"Can we pway hide-an-theek?" she asked, her eyes sparkling.

I giggled in spite of myself and tapped her chin. "Sure."

"Yay!" Rana yelled and shot into action at once, tipping me from my feet so I toppled backwards, stopping myself with one hand.

"I gowing to thee if Maya wanths to pway wif uth," she shouted as she ran back to the house to get Maya.

I stood from my crouching position and sighed. Well, there goes my food. Oh well. Rana was just too cute for her own sake, and even though I had started feeling a bit light-headed from the hunger, I found I just couldn't say no.

After a while, Rana came running back with Maya holding her hand. In no time at all, the three of us were playing hide-and-seek, shouting and running for safety when we were discovered. After the dusk light had faded to grey, the place almost too dark to see anymore, we were called in for dinner.

We were all sitting at the table, the food being passed around.

"Ashley, this is my wife Anne." Nate pointed his finger at the woman who I assumed he had been arguing with a while ago, and I passed the dish of potatoes on without taking anything. They both smiled at me awkwardly, and it was enough to make me stick my hand out for her to shake. "Hello, I'm Ashley."

"Pleasure meeting you," Anne said, taking my hand. Yeah right, *pleasure meeting you*. She didn't know I'd heard her earlier, but it was nothing new having to deal with other peoples' scorn.

"What can I give you to eat?" Anne asked.

"Oh, I'm fine you know, not very hungry." As if in protest, my stomach rumbled so loudly that the others at the table paused mid dish-pass to stare at me or each other.

"Of course you're hungry, it was a long walk to get here. You must be hungry." Nate was frowning, holding his knife and fork a bit too tightly.

Of course I was hungry. Nate was right; it had been a long walk, and I hadn't eaten lunch, but I didn't want to take food that Anne was unwilling to give. I didn't want to be a burden to my family.

"You know I really am fine; just a little tired," I said. "Maybe I should go to bed."

"No, you have to eat first. You must be hungry. You haven't had dinner…" A look of concern crossed Nate's face.

"Honey, leave to poor girl alone," Anne said. "If she's tired, let her go sleep." Of course she would want me to leave, she didn't want to share all this food with me. A pang of hunger stabbed in my stomach, but I tried not to grimace or to drool as I stood from the table and took my eyes off the meat, potatoes, and vegetables. It was even harder than usual to pretend I wasn't hungry, but I managed, even though it seemed like there was plenty of food to go around.

"Yeah, I'll go sleep, I'm pretty tired." The paleness I felt could probably be interpreted as exhaustion. "Goodnight everyone."

I left the room and closed the door behind me. I turned around to continue down to the guest room, but paused when I heard Nate speaking. "Anne, do you really think she's not hungry? Of course she is!" Nate spoke calmly but in an angry voice. "She must have heard you when you were saying that there wasn't enough food for her!"

I sighed and went back to the guest room, collapsing on the bed.

No later than ten minutes after, I heard a small knock on the door. I got to my feet and opened the door, surprised to see Maya standing there.

"Hey, I know you must have heard Mom speaking to Dad about not having enough food for you," she started. "I also know you must be hungry, so I brought a peanut butter sandwich. Also, I'm sorry about my mom. She gets stressed sometimes, but please don't hate her, she's really great when you get to know her. My mom just sometimes worries that one day there won't be enough food for all of us." Maya's chin dipped and she looked at the ground.

I just blinked at her, not knowing what to say. What could I say?

"Here." She handed me the sandwich.

"Uh, thanks," I said.

She smiled at me, and left in a hurry without a glance over her shoulder. That had been such an awkward moment, but for some reason it warmed my heart.

I turned around and closed the door behind me, sitting on the bed. No peanut butter sandwich in the history of peanut butter sandwiches had ever tasted this good, I promise. When it was completely eaten, which was all too soon, I craved more, but considering Anne's strong fears about maybe not having enough to feed everyone, I ignored the growls from my stomach and forced myself to sleep.

SIX

Through the night I dreamed about a baby crying and crying, nobody heard or comforted it. The baby wailed, deep and sorrowful, and I searched for it but couldn't find it. Feelings of fear and confusion floated in my mind, and I woke from the dream with someone shaking me.

"Mom," I muttered, frowning. "One more minute, please!"

"Ashley, get up," Someone—who was definitely not my mom—said.

I shot out of bed at the sound of the new voice. The dream lingered, the sound of a baby crying somewhere far away echoing in my thoughts. I frowned again and rubbed at my eyes. When I looked around everything was unfamiliar. Suddenly I remembered where I was and fell back on my pillow. There was no baby. It had only been a dream.

"Come on, wake up. I need your help!" Someone kept badgering me, pulling at my arm.

I looked up and saw that it was Mark, the ten year old boy.

"What time is it?" I asked.

"It's seven in the morning," he replied, as if it was normal to wake up at such an ungodly hour.

"What do you mean seven in the morning?" I stuffed my face into the pillow and groaned. I usually stayed in bed till nine.

"You have to come and help me," Mark whispered.

"Just a few more hours," I answered.

"Please, Aunt Ashley, I need your help." The 'aunt' bit got me and I instantly sat up. I had a family; nieces and nephews. A brother. It was weird to think that I was an aunt, but when he said that I just found I couldn't resist helping him.

"Okay Mark, what do you need help with?" I flopped my legs over the bed's edge and rubbed at my face again. My hair stood in tufts and drool had dried on my cheek.

"Well, could you just come with me and then I'll tell you?" He used his puppy eyes. How could I say no to those adorable eyes?

"Urgh, fine!" I got up and shuffled to the mirror so I could wrangle some form of decency from the horror staring back at me.

"Yay!" Mark whisper-shouted as he ran from the guest room. "I'll wait for you outside," he quickly added.

I looked at the desk and saw some clothes laid out on it, as well as a note.

The note read:

These are some clothes that you can use since you weren't able to bring yours.
Maya

Maya must have put these here when I was asleep. That was so thoughtful of her. For some reason that little gesture brought a tear to my eye and I had to swallow a wave of deep feelings. What was going on with me? I wasn't usually this mushy.

I quickly dressed, tamed my hair and overall appearance, and slipped outside easily…because no one was awake yet. When I walked outside, I saw Mark sitting on the front porch.

"Okay, what can I help you with?" I smiled at him and he smiled back, a conniving smile.

"I need your help pranking Cynthia and Leah." The smile became even more sneaky, and I laughed.

"It's important," he said. "I must avenge myself."

Avenge. Oh boy. I rolled my eyes.

"They said I look like a girl batman." His expression became insolent. "And I was wearing my batman costume!"

"So let me get this straight. You want to do this just because Leah and Cynthia said that you don't look good in your batman costume?"

"Exactly!" Mark replied and then explained his plan.

"Look, I don't think this is a good idea, we might get in trouble." I tried to reason with Mark but he wasn't giving in.

"No! They offended my batman awesomeness. I will get revenge!" Mark's voice had warped into a younger raspy version of the batman on TV's voice, and I wasn't sure whether it freaked me out or made me want to laugh.

"Okay," I said.

We walked through the trees together. "Can I just ask you why you need me to help with this?" I asked.

"Well, I'm not allowed to go into the forest alone, so I need you to come with me," he started. "I could have woken someone else up, but since I never got to spend time with my aunt, I thought we could do this together." As he finished he looked away.

"Awe, you're so cute"—I ruffled his hair—"I'm also glad to spend time with my nephew." I gave him my biggest smile, and an honest one right then. My nephew! Wow! Another tear threatened to spill at the corner of my eye, and my cheeks started aching with the big smile stretching them wider than they were used to going. I couldn't remember ever being this happy.

"So is everyone like you and Maya? I mean, you guys really aren't shy and you're both really friendly."

"Ew no, please don't compare me to Maya, I'm way awesomer than her, but yeah, we all heard about you and so I was really excited. We don't usually have that much people over, plus, an aunt! That's just awesome!" He said with a cheeky grin. I smiled down at him and bit my lip. This kid was awesome. One thought stayed with me as we walked deeper into the forest. He said that he had heard about me. From who? Nate? And what did he say about me?

"Okay," Mark said, "we're here." We stopped in front of a large pond. A chill shivered up my spine. A flash of blonde hair and blood mixed with a flurry of movement. Sara. A wave of fear spilled over me and I ran to the muddy bank of the pond and splashed water on my face. My fingers trembled as I lifted my hair away and I told myself it was just me feeling nervous about my new family. It had nothing to do with what I had done to Sara. Nothing at all.

When I looked behind me, Mark looked a bit paler, a bit concerned. I forced a smile on my face and said, "I'm fine." He seemed to calm at that and stepped closer to me.

The pond in the early morning light was beautiful. The sun had just peeked over the horizon, its light dappled through tree leaves making a reflection in the water, and there were beautiful flowers all around the pond. All the flowers were different colors.

"Come on, we need to get the frogs!" Mark exclaimed impatiently.

So we got the frogs.

"Are you sure they won't wake up?" I whispered to Mark.

"Not even an elephant could wake them up." Mark said in a matter-of-fact voice.

"Okay, if you say so," I said, not bothering to whisper anymore.

Mark quietly slipped the frogs into Leah and Cynthia's beds, then bolted out of the room with me following.

We ran to the kitchen where Nate and Dylan –the video game kid- sat chatting and making coffee. When we passed them, we tried to act casual.

"Good morning," Nate called after us, "where have you two been?"

"Nowhere!" Mark and I blurted at the same time. We glanced at each other and then we both turned to Nate and smiled with as much innocence as we could muster.

It was weird that I felt so comfortable with people that I barely knew.

"Okay..." Nate stared at me for a second, turned to look at Mark, then turned back to me again. "After you eat breakfast, I want to talk to Ashley alone for a whi-" he was cut off by the sound of screaming.

"There are frogs in our beds!" One of the twins screamed, while the other just squealed in a high pitched voice. The twins were in the kitchen in less than five seconds, disheveled and frantic.

Mark and I had to bite our lips to keep from laughing as the twins jumped on the table, knocking down a few plates in the process.

Now I understand why Mark put the frog in the twins' beds'. The twins were obviously terrified of frogs. I, for one, would not freak out if I woke up with a frog in my bed, seeing as I thought frogs were cute.

"How did frogs get in your be-" Nate stopped talking to look at me and Mark suspiciously. "Do you guys have any idea how frogs got in their beds?"

"What?" I said. "Pfft, no!" Nate drilled into Mark and I with his eyes, but we kept our innocent faces on and after a few seconds he sighed.

"Okay," Nate said, "I'll go get the frogs out of your room. You girls stay here."

"I'll help," Dylan said looking amused. As they left the kitchen Dylan looked back and winked at Mark. We burst out laughing just as the door swung closed, but quickly covered our mouths with our hands. The twins were on the table, hugging each other and looking like they were about to cry. Mark and I discreetly high fived when the twins weren't looking.

I could get used to mornings like this.

SEVEN

"Okay, so Ash- can I call you Ash?" Nate asked.

I nodded.

"Ash, we have a few things to cover here, don't we."

We were currently in Nate's office, only him and I—no children. Considering the mischief Mark and I had caused, it felt awkward sitting alone with Nate, like I might get in trouble at any moment. I had to admit breakfast had been amazing. I had had a plateful of eggs and bacon, the twins had kept giving Mark the evil eye, and I had laughed more than I could remember having laughed in one day.

"First of all, I want to tell you how happy I am that you're here, and that I get to see my sister again." He started smiling, a warmth in his eyes. "But I want to know if you want to stay. Of course if you stay, it will only be till your adoptive parents come back… unless we make arrangements, that is. But we'll talk about that later. Now, what I want to know is if you want to stay at least till your parents come back. It's completely up to you, if you want to go back now, we'll take you back." He finished off with a hint of sadness and his arms folded in front of him.

If I stayed, I would get to know my family better, and maybe learn more about my past. If I left, I would have to go back to my aunt and uncle's house. Also, I didn't know what had happened to Sara. She was the reason I ran away. I should have called for help. I knew nothing serious could have happened to her; when I was thinking that I had killed her, I was being dramatic. She probably just went unconscious for a while, that's all.

But I had still hurt her. Even if we didn't like each other, she was my cousin. So if I went back, I could see if she was okay and I could apologize, but then if I went back she would make my life miserable, and I wouldn't do anything to defend myself out of fear of hurting her again. I should never have pushed her in the first place, but she made me so angry. I saw the locket flying through the air, making a "plop" as it hit the water's surface and sank beneath. The anger boiled in me anew. I wouldn't go back. Not ever if I could help it.

Then again, if I stayed, Aunt Suzy and Uncle Tom would get worried and call the police, if they hadn't already. If they called the police, my parents and brother would come home early from their trip to Italy, so there would be no point in staying. But if I left just when I had finally found my brother, I would regret it all my life. But if I- urgh! I was just confusing myself more. I knew I had to do what my heart was telling me.

Even though these people were strangers, I trusted them, they were my family after all. I didn't need their DNA to know that. I just felt it in some weird beyond the natural way. Besides, they had given me proof: the picture. I knew the picture could be fake or photo-shopped, but I knew it wasn't. Deep down, I just knew.

I needed to stay here to find out more about my parents, about my brother and his children. That's what my heart wanted. I would find a way to tell Aunt Suzy and Uncle Tom that I would be away for a while. Without another thought, I turned to look at my brother.

"I'm staying."

The next day, some of us were going to my aunt and uncle's house so that we could leave a note saying not to call the police, blah, blah, blah. We would say that I was with a friend and that my adoptive parents knew about it. I would have called them, but Nate was scared that they would track the phone and find the house. I really had no idea why that scared him so much. In fact, I found it rather weird that Nate's house was in the middle of nowhere.

Anne –Nate's wife, Rana, Mark, the twins, and Dylan were not coming with us. Anne was feeling sick, and so she decided to stay at home with Rana and the others.

We were half way there, trekking through the forest, when Maya started talking. "So, what happened exactly to make you run into the forest?" she asked, looking at me.

I looked at my feet. "Umm, well"—I cleared my throat—"uh hum."

"Oh, um, you don't have to tell me if you don't want to," Maya quickly said.

In a rush I blurted out what had happened leaving no pause between my words and rushing through it all in one breath. I was too nervous to speak clearly and I hoped that the meaning would get lost in translation. "Well I got angry because Sara threw the only picture that I had of my real parents in a pond I pushed her because I was angry and she got hurt so I ran away."

"Huh?" Maya asked, looking really confused.

I spoke slower this time, reluctantly. She was my niece, and even though it was hard for me to speak about this, maybe it was good having family to tell. Maybe it would help me deal with the pain and confusion of it all. "I got angry because Sara –my cousin– threw the only picture that I had of my real parents in a pond, so I pushed her, and she got hurt, I was scared and ran away."

"Oh..." she trailed off, glanced around us while holding the straps of her backpack. Leaves crunched under our feet to fill the silence.

"Yeah," I said after a minute. "I was really mad because it was a heart locket that my parents left for me with a picture of them inside, and it was the only thing that I had from them."

I suddenly remembered that Nate, Kyle, and Josh were with us, so I turned to look at them. Kyle and Josh were talking walking behind us, speaking and seemingly ignoring us, but Nate seemed to have heard us. He had his fists clenched tightly, and he looked straight ahead.

"Which pond was that?" Maya asked.

As we walked I turned to face her. "It's the pond that you see right before you enter the forest, so we'll probably see it when we're out of the forest. It's pretty hard to miss."

The walk took another hour or two, and by then we were all panting and sweaty. Nate had brought water bottles stashed into his backpack and we shared drinks. He had also packed snacks into a backpack that Maya was carrying, and I devoured two packs of chips as we walked the last bit to the edge of the forest. Ahead of us was the pond. I paused, afraid. This is where I had hurt Sara. Was she really okay? Were the cops looking for me now? I thought about my locket lying at the bottom of the pond, mud swirling around it, and my heart felt cold.

"That's the pond," I told Maya, pointing at the pond that Sara had dropped my locket in. Her eyes were wide as she stared at it, and Nate nodded once. He had definitely heard.

"Oh," Maya said, she paused another few seconds, then started walking again, and the rest of us followed. We walked past the pond, up and down a few streets, and eventually arrived at my aunt and uncle's house. I was surprised to see that their car wasn't there. Well, the job would be easier now. No need to snoop around and hope they didn't see us.

We went to the back door, which my aunt and uncle always left open, and quickly slipped into the house.

"Where do we put the note?" I asked

"Where would your aunt and uncle always be, somewhere where they're sure to see it?" Nate asked, clutching the envelope.

I thought a second, when suddenly I got an idea.

"The TV room." I said. "They always watch TV at night." My uncle never missed his 7 PM news and then his game show afterward. They would definitely see it if we left it on the TV.

I quickly went to the kitchen, which was right next to the TV room, telling everyone to wait for me in the hallway. I opened a few cupboards till I finally found the tape. I ran to the TV room, smiling as I passed by everyone in the hallway. I walked to the TV and stuck the note onto its screen with tape on all four corners. Just in case, I taped the remote itself onto the TV screen too, right next to the note. There was no way they would miss it now. I was heading out of the room when I heard something strange behind me. I had turned the television on by mistake. I looked up and saw that it was the news channel. That was weird, considering the fact that my uncle always watched the game show before sleeping, not the news channel. I gasped as I saw the heading on the TV. It said 'Young girl missing and another found half dead.'

Below it was a reporter talking:

"A teenager, Ashley Jones, has gone missing and her cousin, Sara Jones, was found severely injured and unconscious by a pond near a forest. No one knows who—or what—has hurt her, because the young girl is still unconscious and cannot tell us what happened, and no one knows if Ashley was taken by the person or animal that injured Sara. Mr. Daniels, the hero who has found the girl, says that he was going hunting when he came across the girl. No one knows what has happened to her, but whatever or whoever injured her is dangerous…"

I felt dizzy suddenly and fell back into the couch. I was not dangerous! She was the one who had hurt me. But she was still unconscious. I hadn't hurt her that bad, had I?

"Come on, we have to go." Josh pulled me out of my thoughts with a friendly smile as he peeked back into the doorway.

"Just catching my breath," I said. I stood up and turned the TV off before walking back into the hallway.

We used the opportunity of an empty house for bathroom breaks, to my relief, and once we were all fresh, we headed back to the forest. I was deep in thought, fears for Sara and my future if they found out I had hurt her warred with anger at her actions and a feeling of injustice that I had had to grow up with people who hated me so much, who pushed me to this kind of extreme action. The walk back to the house started off very silently.

I couldn't believe that Sara had been unconscious for twenty four hours or more. I sighed deeply through my nose.

"So umm," Maya started, obviously trying to make conversation. "Do you like cows?" she blurted.

I stared at her.

"I mean cows can be cool sometimes, like they provide milk for us, but they're also annoying. I mean they poop everywhere. And they always have flies covering them, you know what I mean? Though their eyes are so cute and big, and when they moo they just look so adorable, but then it gets annoying after a while, because they moo all the time and—"

"Be quiet!" Josh said, making Maya instantly stop.

Josh looked at me, laughing a little when he saw my face.

My eyes were wide, and my mouth was slightly open. What in the world? How could someone possibly talk so fast?

"She gets like that when she doesn't know what to say," Kyle – the one who had helped Josh get me—explained.

"Okay..." I trailed off awkwardly.

"I'm so sorry. That happens a lot," Maya said, looking worried. Why was she worried?

"It's fine, why do you look so worried?" I voiced my thoughts, frowning.

"I just don't want you to think I'm weird," Maya mumbled.

"Too late for that," I heard Kyle snicker, bringing a laugh bubbling from my chest.

"Don't worry, I think we're all weird in a way. There's no one in the world that's normal, I mean, what is the definition of normal? It's impossible to be normal," I stated. "Oh, and to answer your question, I don't like cows."

Maya blushed, looking away.

"Do you want to know why?" I asked, not wanting her to be embarrassed.

Maya shook her head and looked away, fiddling with her backpack strap.

"Once, I went to a farm and I stepped in cow poop. I tried to take it off my shoe by scrubbing it with a sponge, but it wouldn't work, so my brother—Andrew—took my shoe to his room to take the poop off, and it worked. When I asked him how he had done it, he said that he had used my toothbrush to scrub it off."

Maya, Josh, and Kyle burst out laughing, but when I looked at Nate, I saw that he looked angry and...sad? Was that what it was?

I suddenly realized that I had talked about Andrew for the first time, referring to him as my brother. I shrugged it off, and continued talking to Maya, Josh, and Kyle all the way back to their house. Nate was quiet and brooding all the way, his fists clenching and unclenching every now and then, his jaw working as if he was biting back a filthy word. Josh and Kyle kept shooting him worried looks but they acted nonchalant and continued their conversation throughout the whole walk.

When I got to the guest room, I sat on the bed and started to think of the report on the news again.

Was I dangerous?

Although Maya had cheered me up, I still couldn't forget what the reporter had said on the news. Of course I had hurt her! I felt my palms pushing against her shoulders and looked at my hands.

This was not like in movies or in books, where everyone had a thousand lives and never got hurt in fights. This was the real world.

Once, on the news, I heard about a boy who had died because someone had punched him. Died. Now I was the culprit, the… I shuddered as I thought it. The murderer.

The guilt grew and grew inside me, and for the umpteenth time I was crying, tears spilling from my eyes and tapping onto the sheets. I hadn't meant to hurt Sara, not really. I had just been angry about what she'd done. It still made me angry to think about it, but now it made me afraid too, to think of what I might have done because of a locket. The angry part of me wanted to justify my actions, but deep down, the guilty part kept nudging me into sorrow. Was I dangerous? Evil? Was I…was I a murderer?

Thinking about the locket also got me thinking about my parents, what they might have been like. Was my mother as brave as I had always imagined? I wanted to go talk to Nate; to ask about my past, but I was worried that he wouldn't want to talk about the past. What if asking him evoked bad memories? I shook my head. Why would there be any bad memories? Wiping my eyes, I reluctantly got up and went to his office. I paused for a nervous second before knocking.

"Come in!" Nate called out.

I opened the door and stood awkwardly in the doorway, my arms folded over my chest. Were my eyes puffy? I wiped at my face again, just in case.

Nate looked up from his desk, concerned. "Sit down, sit down." He gestured to the chair on the other side of the desk and I walked over with my head down.

I sat down hesitantly, and looked at my brother. My brother! I guess I still hadn't grasped the concept that I had a biological brother; a brother related to me genetically, and attached to me with some invisible beyond natural chord of familiarity.

"So sis, how can I help you?" Nate asked.

I stared at him in a daze. He called me sis. Sis! As in sister! I had a brother, and he called me sis. We were related! We had the same parents! I was his sister! He was my brother! He knew my—our—parents, and he could tell me more about them! I was his sis. I smiled.

"Uh...are you okay?" Nate asked, tapping his pen on the desk, an honest look of concern on his face. I realized that I had just been staring at him instead of answering.

"Um, ye-yeah. Yeah I'm fine," I quickly answered and tried to make my smile a bit bigger, a bit more genuine.

"I wanted to ask you if-" I was cut off by the door opening.

"Dylan, as you can see I'm trying to talk to Ashley, so if yo-" Dylan cut him off. "It's Maya, we can't find her anywhere."

EIGHT

As soon as Nate and I heard those words, we shot up from our chairs.

"What!" I cried. "Where did you look?"

"Since when has she been missing?" Nate asked quietly as he stood, hands in his pockets, a determined gleam in his eye.

"We looked everywhere," Dylan answered. "She went missing right after you guys arrived back home, and that was three hours ago!"

"Three hours!" Nate and I shouted together.

Had we been back for three hours already? Wow, time passed so quickly!

"Well, umm, maybe she's..." I trailed off, not knowing what to say. Wait! She might be with her friends. "At her friend's house!" I exclaimed enthusiastically.

"She doesn't have any friends," Dylan said. "Since we're home schooled we don't really meet a lot of people, and we live in the middle of nowhere."

Oh, that's why I hadn't seen any friends around.

"Why are you so worried? Doesn't she ever go for a walk in the forest or something?" I asked.

"Well yeah, but never alone, and she always tells us first." Nate explained.

"Okay, does she have a phone?" I asked.

"Yes, but she's not answering!" Dylan answered.

"So let's go search for her." I said.

We all left Nate's office to search for Maya. We searched all over the house; in Maya, Dylan, Josh, Kyle, the twins, Mark, and Rana's rooms, in the kitchen, the living room, the TV room, the guest room, Nate and Anne's room...but we still couldn't find her.

We then searched outside to see if we could find her, but we didn't. I could see the panic in Nate's eyes. We went into the forest searching for her, but the forest was so big that she could have been anywhere. We shouted her name, ranging the forest within sight of each other, Nate calling out loudest. After hours of searching in the forest, I sat down on the grassy ground. Where was she? I was really getting worried.

At first I hadn't been *that* worried because three hours wasn't that much, but now it had been five hours since we last saw her and everyone was panicking.

What if she had been kidnapped? What if she had been taking a walk, and tripped and hurt herself? Just as I was thinking this, I saw Maya walking right up to us, her clothes soaking wet and a huge smile on her face.

"Where have you been?" I shouted at Maya, who was practically skipping towards us.

She smiled. "Oh, you know, around..."

Nate saw her and shouted angrily at Maya as he ran closer. "Around! Around? That's what you say? Do you know how worried we were?"

"Well there was just something I had to do..." Maya trailed off.

The other had heard by now and gathered, running closer from where they had been searching. Maya looked worried for a second and then she sighed. As the twins arrived they pummeled into her, not caring that she was wet.

Nate frowned. "Young lady, you have exactly two minutes to explain where you were, or else..." He paused for a second, obviously not knowing what to say. "Or else, I'll- I'll, umm, take your phone away?" It sounded more like a question than a threat, and I could see he was relieved.

"We never do anything bad so our parents don't know how to punish us," Leah explained and bumped her shoulder against Maya's. At least I think it was Leah, I'm not sure. Maybe it was Cynthia…oh well, I would just find out later.

"Dad, there was just something I had to do, I'm very sorry for not telling you that I was leaving." Maya looked down and a blush colored her cheeks. "Please forgive me, it won't happen again."

I saw Nate's eyes soften further. "Fine, but if you ever leave without telling me again, you'll be punished." Some people would have said that he was being overprotective, but I think that he just cared a lot and I found that very sweet.

"Though you still have to explain why you're so wet," Nate said.

"I tripped into a puddle," Maya answered. Water dripped from her nose and tapped steadily from the edge of her shirt.

Of course Nate didn't believe her, no one did. It was obvious that she was lying. It looked as though Nate was about to add something, but then he just let it slide, obviously tired of arguing with his daughter.

"What do you guys say we go back inside?" Kyle suggested.

We all nodded in agreement and headed back towards the house, Maya dripping right next to me. I nudged her shoulder and smiled. "I'm glad you're okay."

It was late that night when I heard a knock on the door to the guest room. Who would be there at this time of night? I had stayed up thinking about the last two days, trying to forget Sara and wondering what Maya had been doing.

"Come in," I said in a hushed tone.

The door opened, and I came face to face with Maya.

"Hey," she said, her hands behind her back.

"Hey," I answered. "Do you need anything?"

She smiled again, and for a brief moment I thought that this might be how it felt to have a sister. "Yeah, actually I wanted to give you something," Maya said.

What would she want to give me? And at this hour?

Maya took her hands out and placed something in my hand.

I looked at what she placed in my hand, and my heart started racing in my chest, my breaths coming quicker. "My locket?" I could barely get the words out. It was my locket! The one that Sara had thrown in the lake. The one that my biological parents had placed with me when they left me in front of the orphanage. The locket felt cold and I curled my hands around it to reassure myself that it was still there, that it was real.

"Wh- what, how?" I couldn't get words out. My heart was still pounding away at my chest.

"Well, when I left earlier, it was to get you the locket. Since I'm a good swimmer, and I wanted to make you happy, I went to the pond to get it for you." Maya shrugged, then looked over her shoulder.

"How is that possible?" I asked, still stunned.

"I am quite a good swimmer," she said. "I just went in the pond you showed me, and since I can hold my breath for a long time, I was able to feel the bottom of the pond. I felt the bottom of the pond till I found your locket. The pond was pretty dirty, so I couldn't see; that's why it took me a long time to get back." She walked closer and sat on the edge of the bed next to me.

"Why didn't you tell the others about it?" I whispered, brushing my thumb lightly against the silver.

"Well, I know it's probably special to you, and I know that you wouldn't want everyone knowing about what happened with you and your cousin, so I just kept quiet about it." She shrugged again and tears spilled from my eyes. I hugged her long and tight and tried not to wet her again with all the tears.

"Thank you," I said into her shoulder. She just squeezed tighter.

After a while I leaned back to look into her eyes. "Thank you. Really. This is-" I had wanted to say the most important thing in the world to me, but now that I had her and Nate—actual family—I suppose that wasn't true anymore.

"No problem," Maya said. "I want you to be happy." She smiled and waved as she walked out of the guest room, leaving me feeling shell-shocked. And I felt something else, something I had never truly felt before. I felt loved.

NINE

I woke up to a bright light shining on my face. I rolled over in my bed, aiming to get my legs on the side of the bed and to land gracefully on my feet. Well, no. That wasn't going to happen; not this early in the morning. As I tried to get my feet off the bed, I slipped and face planted the floor instead. Yeah, that's what actually happened. So there I was, rolling and groaning on the floor in pain, when someone entered the guest room.

"Rise and shi-" the voice paused as the person looked at me. "Maybe this isn't a good time. I think I'll come back later."

"Wait!" I groaned and reached towards the closing door.

I heard footsteps approaching me and soon saw a hand in front of my face.

Me being me, I declined the offer and tried to stand up by myself, using the bed sheet to pull myself up. Success? Nope. All I did was half stand up using the bed sheet for help until it slid off the bed, making me fall again with the sheet covering me.

I could hear laughing coming from the person who had tried to offer me a hand.

I kicked my legs out in the bed sheet, trying to find an exit.

"Let me help you," the voice offered.

After trying to free myself for what seemed like hours, the bed sheet was off and I could finally see again. I looked up and my eyes landed right on Josh's face.

"Here, let me help you stand up," Josh offered, putting his hand in front of my face again.

I shook my head, not wanting help. It must have been the confined space and the falling around like that first thing in the morning, but I felt nervous suddenly. Just as I was about to stand up, Josh quickly grabbed my wrist and pulled me up.

Before I could scold him for helping me, he quickly said, "We don't have all day, and you obviously can't stand up by yourself so I helped you. Don't complain please, and come with me so we can eat breakfast."

Shoving him out of the way, I jogged to the bathroom. As if things hadn't been embarrassing enough, now I was running away like a crazy person, but I needed to pee and I could feel a sticky patch of drool on my cheek. So embarrassing! When I got to the bathroom I heard the sounds of someone puking and reluctantly decided I'd have to hold it in till a bit later.

When we arrived to the kitchen, I saw that everyone was already eating. Josh and I quickly sat down in our places. Anne came in just after us, wiping her mouth and rubbing her forehead.

"Help yourself," Anne told me, but she looked pale as she glanced at the eggs on the table and I noticed she didn't grab a plate to eat with us. I remembered what I had overheard her say to her husband; how there wasn't enough food to feed me. Although I didn't want to take any food, I saw Nate looking at me and I didn't want to upset him.

I took some toast and jam, and ate it slowly. My stomach roared at me and I wanted to wolf down another slice of toast, but I held back. The uneasy feeling returned as I sat chewing nervously.

Soon everyone was done, and we were talking about what we

were going to do today.

"So, what are the plans for today?" I asked everybody.

"Today," Cynthia (I think it was Cynthia) paused dramatically, "we take you exploring."

We were going exploring without Nate and Anne. Just all the kids, except Rana, who had to stay at home because she was too young to come with us. Anne was still feeling sick, and she hadn't gotten time to object from the bathroom where she was puking her guts out. I kind of felt bad for her, but she insisted she was okay, and Rana was standing with her, holding Anne's hair up and clutching her teddy in the other hand.

We walked into the forest and started talking.

"So, where are you taking me?" I asked everyone.

"We're taking you to our secret area," Cynthia explained (I think it was Cynthia—this was getting confusing).

Secret area? What did she mean by that? I guessed I'd just have to find out. "How come you call this exploring?" I asked everyone, slightly confused.

"Oh, we just said that because we were in front of mom and dad. They don't know about our secret area and we don't want them to know, so we just say we're going exploring every time we want to go to our secret place," Mark explained.

Okay, that made much more sense. The twins giggled and held

each others' hands. Maya walked on my right side, and Josh on my left.

"Hey Ash, do you know what today is?" Josh asked me.

"No, what's today?" I asked curiously.

"Today is game night!" Leah (again, I think) said excitedly.

"Every Friday we have game night, which means that at night, we play many different games! It's kind of like our family time. It's our time to 'bond'—as mom puts it." Maya said, air quoting the word 'bond'.

"Oh cool, that seems fun," I said, a smile on my face.

"No, it's not!" Dylan said. "It's lame! I have other things to do."

"Shut up, Dylan!" Joshua, Kyle, and Mark said at the same time.

"Jinx!" Mark yelled. "You all owe me sodas!" He pointed at them accusingly as we walked.

I laughed a little at his cuteness.

We were walking for a long time, when finally, we stopped in front of...the ground? Seriously, we walked all this way to get to some random place?

"Uh, cool place guys..." I trailed off, not really knowing what to say.

For some reason, when I said that, everyone started laughing. Why? I have absolutely no idea.

"This is not our secret area, dummy!" Maya said, still laughing.

Kyle kneeled down on the floor and pushed away a bunch of dry leaves. Right under all the leaves, there was a long wooden plank with a handle on it. Kyle took the handle and pulled the wooden plank up.

I gasped at what I saw.

There was a wooden ladder than led us underground. I leaned down and took hold of the ground to either side of the opening, then furtively stepped into the gloom. Joshua followed behind me and flicked on a light switch while I stood staring at the darkness trying not to feel afraid. The room was about ten meters long, and at least five meters underground. As I descended, I saw that there was a small table and three beanbags in the room. There were also three chairs. The walls were covered with posters and pictures. All in all, the place was beautiful.

"You guys dug an underground room?" I asked bewildered.

"Well, we didn't exactly build it, we just found it and modified it," Mark explained.

"It took us like three months to improve and modify but it was worth it," Kyle said as he climbed down the ladder.

"Wow!" I said, still breathless.

"Come on inside," Maya called up to Mark and held out her hand to help him down the ladder. When Mark was safely in, Maya pulled the trapdoor closed. Everyone sat down on a beanbag, on a chair, or on the floor. I went and sat down on the floor next to Maya.

"So, you guys basically come here to relax?" I asked, looking around.

"Yeah, when we need a break from Mom and Dad we come here." Leah (was it Leah?) told me. I really needed to be able to tell the difference between Cynthia and Leah, but asking about it now would be embarrassing.

"Wow," I muttered again.

"You have to promise not to tell Mom and Dad though," Dylan quickly said.

"I, Ashley Nadia Jones—uh I mean Coffman, promise to never, ever tell Nate and Anne about this secret underground room," I said and I intended to keep my promise.

"Okay good. Now let's party!" Maya said, tugging a bag of chips out of her backpack.

We talked and ate for a long time, having our own family time. Joshua switched on a little stereo and the twins started dancing with Mark. I smiled at them and sighed contently. I could get used to this.

That night, as everyone had told me, it was game night. We all sat cross-legged on the living room floor, forming a circle. My heart felt warm as I looked around at the faces there, but I tried not to look too eager.

"What do you guys want to play?" Nate asked, looking around.

"How about Uno?" Mark suggested. We all nodded and Dylan gave everyone seven cards. After a few games of Uno (all of which I had lost) we decided to play Monopoly. I laughed as I listened to some stories about Mark when he was a mischievous baby in between turns and tried hard not to giggle as I listened about a time when Leah and Cynthia had pretended to be each other. After about an hour of monopoly, the game ended and I had once again lost. I wasn't really great with games but I was having loads of fun.

"What do you guys want to play now?" Nate asked.

"Let's play 'Would you rather'" Maya said excitedly. "I love that game."

"Sure, why not," Josh said, getting up and going to the kitchen. He soon came back with an empty water bottle.

Joshua sat back down and spun the bottle. It landed on Rana.

"Rana, would you rather, um…" Josh thought for a second. "Be a gummy bear or a gummy worm?"

"A gummy beaw!" Rana yelled happily. "I wuv gummy beawth!"

"Okay Rana, now you spin the bottle," Dylan told her.

Rana spun the bottle and it landed on Maya.

"Would you wather have ninja poweth ow be abal to wead mind?" Rana asked, eyeing Maya with a ferocious intensity.

"Definitely be able to read minds! Well, actually, maybe ninja powers since that would be super cool. No, I would want to read minds so that I could know everything people think." Maya frowned and I stifled a laugh.

Maya spun the bottle and it landed on Dylan.

"Dylan, would you rather have the hiccups for the rest of your life, or have the feeling that you need to sneeze but you're never able to for the rest of your life?" Maya asked.

"Have the feeling that I need to sneeze. I would hate hiccupping for the rest of my life!" Dylan answered, scrunching up his nose.

So the game went on for what seemed like hours until Nate asked me a question that I would never be able to answer. The bottle had scraped to a stop, the room was silent and all eyes were fixed on me.

I looked into Nate's face, all hints of amusement had left his features. "Would you rather have me as a brother, or Andrew?"

TEN

Who was my favorite brother? What an unfair question! My heart started beating fast and my palms became sweaty. I could never answer a question like that. It was too much. I didn't want Nate to think that I didn't like him, but I had only known him for a few days. I had known Andrew my whole life. If I had to choose between them I would choose Andrew. He was my best friend. He was the only one who'd ever loved me before a few days ago. I didn't want to say that to Nate, though. Of course I didn't want to. He kept looking at me and I fidgeted with the hem of my shirt.

"Time for bed kids!" Anne said into the silence, saving me from answering.

"Yeah guys. I'm super tired, let's go to bed now," Maya said, faking a yawn.

"Yeah, yeah. I'm very tired, too," Josh said, standing up.

"But I'm not tiewd," Rana said, not comprehending the situation.

"No, you're going to bed now, it's late and you have that, umm, that…that thing that you have to do tomorrow," Anne said, saving me again.

As everyone was speaking and trying to change the subject, Nate maintained eye contact with me. He looked almost pleading, begging me with his eyes to tell him the answer. I started fidgeting under his gaze. I felt very uncomfortable.

Finally, I also stood up and said, "Yeah, I'm very tired. I'm going to bed now…thank you for letting me play with you guys, I had lots of fun."

I quickly left the living room and went to the guest room. Just before I shut the door, I heard Anne talking angrily. I had to strain my ears to make out what she was saying. "How could you do that?" Anne was saying. "You can't ask a stupid question like that! Do you ever use your brain? Do you ever think? How can you be so childish?"

I honestly don't think he was thinking when he asked me that question. Though I hated to admit it, I understood his curiosity. Sighing, I closed the door behind me, then quickly got dressed in the pajamas that Maya had let me borrow and sat on the bed in the guest room.

What was I going to do tomorrow? Thing would be so awkward. Ugh! Why did Nate ask that question? Why, why, why?

A knock at the door snapped me out of my thoughts. Please don't be Nate, please don't be Nate, please don't be Nate.

"Can we come in?" A voice said. "It's us, Cynthia and Leah."

I sighed in relief. "Yeah, come in," I answered.

The door opened and Cynthia and Leah came into the room. "Hey, how are you?" Cynthia asked.

I shrugged, trying to look casual. "I'm fine. I'm okay."

"I'm very sorry about the question Dad asked you. It wasn't fair," Leah said (I think—gosh this was going to drive me insane—I had to ask them who was who).

"Yeah, it wasn't fair, but I guess he was just curious," I said.

One of the twins nodded. "Yeah, that's true."

We stayed silent for a moment. I leaned my head against the

dashboard of the bed, thinking of something to say.

"Can I ask you guys something? I know it's weird, but…" I leaned my chin on a pillow. "It's just, I can't really tell who is who with you guys." It felt awkward then, and I fumbled my words. "I mean I'm sure you guys get this all the time but I feel so stupid never knowing who is who and I know you guys aren't copies of each other but I just can't tell and I'm sorry if I'm offending you but it's driving me nuts, and"—I paused and met each of their eyes, expecting frowns or scowls, but they were laughing—"and I guess it's very stupid." I said.

"Don't worry about it. I'm Cynthia." Cynthia put her hand on her chest then put four fingers on her forehead. "My forehead is the normal-sized forehead." She started laughing and Leah shoved her over. She kept laughing though and put her hand against Leah's forehead. "See? She has a five-head." Leah frowned and slapped Cynthia's hand away.

"Well I am thinner!" Leah pronounced, standing on the bed and proving it by putting both hands on her hips and squeezing her tummy. Her thumbs nearly touched. "Show her," Leah said, and Cynthia finally stopped laughing. She stood up and copied Leah's stance to the tee. Her fingers were a little further apart than Leah's. She knocked Leah over and proceeded to laugh again. "And I'm the one with the"—she changed her voice—"husky, sexy voice."

Leah laughed and I couldn't help laughing along. "No you're not. You're putting on that voice."

Cynthia bounced back onto the bed and put her arms behind her neck. "But my voice is deeper."

Leah slapped her knee and Cynthia laughed again. They knew just how to lift my mood and they barely knew me.

"So, what do you guys like to do?" I asked them

They seemed a little confused by my question.

"I only know a little about you, now." I pointed to Cynthia. "Four-head" Then to Leah. "Five-head. But I want to know more. What you guys like, what you do. You know." I waved my hand in a flourish.

An understanding look crossed over their faces.

"Okay well, why don't we describe each other?" Leah said. "I'll tell you about Cynthia, and Cynthia can tell you about me."

"Sure." I nodded. "Why don't you start Leah?"

"Well, let me see. Fatty over here plays basketball, she loves bike riding, and she's a very good soccer player. She loves swimming, American football, and climbing trees. She's very blunt and says the first thing that comes to her mind..." Leah was interrupted by Cynthia's complaints.

"I am not blunt!" Cynthia said, pouting.

Leah sighed, faking annoyance.

"As I was saying before I was rudely interrupted," Leah started, fake glaring at Cynthia. "Cynthia is very blunt, she interrupts a lot, she's super clumsy, she can be very sweet when she feels like it, and she's the best sister ever!" Leah finished off, smiling sweetly at her sister.

"Okay, my turn!" She wore a conniving smile. "Five-head loves to read, write, and draw. She loves singing and dancing, and she's always very calm. She's usually very shy, but not with you, Ashley.

She loves to paint, and she's very good at it. In the morning, she usually goes to the forest to sit under the trees and listen to the birds singing. She's always helping people, and she's simply everything I could ever wish for in a sister." Cynthia hugged Leah to her with one arm and Leah blushed.

They were so cute. It was obvious that they loved each other, though they seemed to be opposites.

"Yeah, I know what you're thinking, me and Leah are complete opposites and that's actually true except for one thing, even if we don't want it," Cynthia paused looking at her sister. "We sometimes say the same thing at the same time." I laughed and they laughed with me.

Have you ever laughed on a very bouncy bed? If you have, you might guess what happened next. Cynthia and Leah started hitting each other with pillows, and the laughter started making the bed bounce. Suddenly I was no longer on the bed; I was falling. There was a big *thud* when I hit the ground and the two girls were immediately at my side.

"Oh my gosh! Are you okay?" They asked at the same time, causing me to start laughing hysterically again.

The girls looked at each other with a look that said *'she's crazy'* which made me think of twins and their mysterious telepathic connection, causing me to laugh even harder. My laughing must have been contagious because both girls started laughing with me again, soon joining me on the floor. I bet we looked crazy; me with my face on the floor, and my nieces laughing like maniacs.

Abruptly, the door was pushed open. The person who had

entered started to say something, but stopped when they saw the condition we were in. All on the floor, rolling, holding our tummies, eyes watering with the laughs.

"Umm, girls do you mind going to your rooms for a minute?" It was Anne.

The girls and I sobered up, and stood.

"Yeah sure, we'll go out." They said at the same time. "Stop that!" They yelled at the same time again. They both left the room, leaving me and Anne alone.

Anne closed the door after the twins had left and sat down on the bed. She looked at me and patted the spot next to her. I quickly sat down next to her, biting my nails nervously. I know I was laughing a minute ago, but now, with Anne here, I suddenly remembered the question that Nate had asked me.

"Are you okay?" Anne asked, surprising me.

"Uh yeah, I'm fine." I answered.

"Look, I apologize for Nate's question. He wasn't thinking. I'm very, very sorry," Anne said, surprising me again.

"Um yeah, it's fine," I said, shrugging.

Anne nodded and stood up, walking to the door. Just before she reached the door, she paused and turned around. She walked back to the bed and stopped when she was right in front of me.

"Also, I wanted to say that I'm sorry for what I said. I know you probably heard me telling Nate that we don't have enough food, and that's why you didn't eat anything that first day. I'm so sorry, I didn't mean any of that. Please forgive me," she said, making me totally speechless. She was apologizing to me? Really? This was a weird day.

Anne was staring at me and I realized that she was waiting for my answer.

"Yes, I forgive you," I told her.

"Thank you," she said, and for the millionth time that day, she surprised me by hugging me. I simply hugged her back and patted her back awkwardly.

Anne finally pulled away and walked to the door.

"Good night, Ashley." She said just before closing the door.

Maya had be right; Anne was kind once you got to know her. Even though we had gotten off on the wrong foot, I think now we were on good terms.

I started walking to the bed but then I spun around and tiptoed down stairs to the kitchen. I opened a few cupboards till I found a pack of barbeque chips. I grabbed them and quickly went back to my room –well, the guest room. I opened the pack of chips and smiled as the amazing aroma reached my nose. What can I say? I sure do love food.

The next morning, I woke up not remembering anything that had happened the day before. I quickly got dressed and got ready to go to the kitchen for breakfast. As I was walking to the kitchen, the previous day's events flooded back into my mind. I grunted in annoyance. What was I going to do? When I finally arrived in front of the kitchen door, I paused and braced myself for the awkwardness. I didn't want to go in there! I sighed and open the door despite the fact that I wanted to turn around and go back to the guest room. When I entered the kitchen, I was surprised to see Dylan, the twins, Kyle, Rana, Anne, Josh, and Mark, but no Nate or Maya.

"Good morning honey, what would you like for breakfast?" Anne asked sweetly. She looked better today, at last. She had been sick for a while now.

"Toast would be great," I said, not refusing this time since Anne and I were on good terms and my stomach was growling furiously at me.

Anne put some toast in my plate and piled on scrambled eggs. I frowned a bit at the memory of Aunt Suzy and her disgusting eggs but then I quickly covered it up with a smile.

"Thank you," I said.

"No problem," Anne said wearing a sweet smile.

I dribbled some ketchup over the lot and wolfed it down one fork at a time, though my stomach still felt half empty when I was done. Anne seemed just as hungry as me, and it was good to see her eating after being sick for so long.

I looked at Josh hesitantly between bites, debating internally whether I should ask the questions that I had on my mind. Soon my curiosity got the best of me and I asked, the words rushing from my mouth. "Josh, do you, uh- do you know where Nate is?"

"Yeah," he said slowly, "He went to get some groceries with Maya."

"Oh, okay," I said, sighing defiantly. I had to face him at some point, but I was relieved it wasn't now.

"Do you guys want to play video games?" Dylan asked, trying to lighten the mood.

"Yeah! Sure!" Josh answered.

"Mom, can we go or do you need help in the kitchen?" Leah asked.

"No, it's fine I don't need any help. All of you can go, except Rana." Anne pointed to Rana with her fork.

"No mommy! I wanna go! Pwease!" Rana said, using her puppy eyes.

"Rana, I am your mom and you obey me," Anne ordered sternly. "I said you're staying, so you stay. You need to be practicing your reading."

Rana huffed angrily but went to her mother anyways.

She was just too cute!

"Okay, we'll be upstairs in my room Mom," Dylan said, obviously trying not to laugh at Rana and Anne's little episode. Dylan walked out of the kitchen, soon followed by the rest of us. We walked up some stair which I've never seen before and turner to the second door to the right. Dylan pushed open the door, and the room that I saw amazed me.

The room was huge and painted a dark, sea blue. There was a very fluffy looking carpet that was also blue, probably to match the walls. There was a double bed with a blue comforter and a few white pillows. There were three blue bean-bags right next to the bed. There was a huge TV set on a wall facing the double bed. There was an Xbox, a Playstation, and a Wii placed on a small shelf next to the TV. One wall was filled with pictures; many, many different pictures. Right next to the bed was a medium sized, wooden desk. All in all, the room was beautiful, and once again I began to wonder how it was possible for people with such a beautiful house to be short on money.

The twins each sat on a bean-bag and everyone else sat on the huge bed. I went and sat on the remaining bean-bag, looking at everyone to see what we would do next.

"Okay guys, what do you want to play?" Dylan asked.

"Umm, can we play Call of Zombies?" Mark asked.

"No! Why don't we play Unicorn Land?" Leah asked.

"Really, Leah? Unicorn Land?" Cynthia said, clearly irritated.

"Lay off! I'm just kidding, I don't even know if that's actually a game!" Leah said defensively.

"Why don't we play Mario Cart?" Kyle asked. That's when I realized he was here. Wow, he was very quiet. He almost never talked.

"Yeah, that's a good idea!" Josh agreed.

Dylan stood up and went to a pile of discs stacked on his desk. He looked through them for a while and finally took one out of the pile. He went to the Wii, placed the disc inside, turned on the TV and went back to his desk, opening a drawer. He then took out four Wii remote controls and handed one to Cynthia, Mark, Kyle, and me.

"We'll take turns." He said before setting up the game.

"I have to win!" Mark shouted, tilting his remote to the side, making his car turn abruptly to the right. He had chosen Maria as his character. Who did I have? Rosalina! Just my luck.

"You're not going to win because I'm gonna beat to you!" Kyle said, also turning his remote to the right, causing his car to hit Mark's car. He turned his arms with his remote, causing his whole body to go to the right, almost making him fall off the bed.

We played for about an hour before deciding to go back downstairs. We arrived downstairs just as Nate arrived home...alone.

Anne walked out of the hallway and went up to Nate.

"Um, honey? Where's Maya?" she asked nervously.

"Maya? She didn't come with me," he answered, his brows pressed together in confusion.

"What? When I saw that she wasn't here, I assumed that she had gone with you." Anne said, a trickle of sweat falling from her forehead. Her shoulders tensed, as did her jaw.

"No! She didn't!"

"Let's just call her." Anne suggested.

Cynthia took her phone out of her pocket and dialed a number. After a minute of it ringing she took the phone away from her ear.

"No answer." She said.

Nate's face started wrinkling with worry before he suddenly relaxed and the wrinkles left without a trace. "Let's not start getting worried for nothing; Maya probably just went out for a walk like she did the other day. Let's just wait, she'll eventually show up."

Anne's shoulders sagged and her whole face relaxed. "Yeah, you're right! Let's just wait."

And wait we did. For five hours.

"Guys, it's been five hours. Don't you think we should maybe go look for her?" I asked, worried. I had been in my room trying to avoid going downstairs to prevent awkwardness with Nate, but now I was really worried about Maya.

"Yeah, maybe we should," Nate agreed.

"Let's search in groups," Nate said. "Me and Ashley together, the twins with Dylan, Mark with Josh and Kyle, and Anne honey, maybe you should stay at home with Rana in case Maya shows up here."

What? We were together? This was going to be weird. I guess Nate wanted to talk to me. I sighed as everyone agreed. Okay, this was going to be an awkward search. We all went outside and broke into our different groups, me with Nate.

"So, um, I wanted to apologize for the question that I asked yesterday," Nate said, getting straight to the point.

"Uh yeah, it's fine," I said, a little nervous.

Nate sighed and bit his lip. There was an awkward silence for a few minutes. We could only hear the sound of our footsteps on the forest ground, crushing a few leaves, as we searched for Maya. Nate finally broke the silence by asking me a question.

"So, just wondering, what's your middle name?"

What a weird question!

"My middle name's Nadia," I said hesitantly.

As I said that, something weird flickered in Nate's eyes.

"Okay Ashley, you wanted to know more about your past, so I'll tell you more." Nate said, surprising me.

"Okay..." I answered excitedly but nervously at the same time.

Nate hadn't yet brought up the conversation about my past and now I was a little worried. My heartbeat increased and my palms became sweaty. Breathe in, breathe out, breathe in, breathe out, bre...

"Nadia is actually your real name," Nate said. "Mom chose it. Your name was changed when you were adoption." He had stopped walking and looked at me intensely, waiting for my reaction.

My breathing became fast and my head started hurting. Was that true? Was Nadia my real name? *Breathe in, breathe out, breathe in, breathe out.* My whole life, I had thought my name was Ashley, when my name had actually been Nadia. *Ashley, don't freak out, don't freak out, don't freak out!*

How was this possible? First, I find out that I'm adopted, then I deal with adoptive parents that don't care about me, then I find out that I have blood relatives, and now I find out that my name isn't even my name. The only thing that was true, the only thing I thought I knew about myself; a lie. My only way to identify myself, I wasn't just 'the daughter of people who put me up for adoption' or 'the adopted daughter of people who didn't care'; I was Ashley, the girl who was who she wanted to be, the girl who wasn't defined by her past. I was my own self, my own character. I was Ashley. But this whole time, I hadn't even been Ashley. It was just another lie to add to the list. Tears began to fall from my eyes and I bit my lip to stop myself from whimpering.

My thinking was cut off by a scream. Nate and I abruptly turned in the direction of the scream and quickly ran towards it. I wiped my eyes as we ran, not wanting anyone to see that I was crying. When we arrived we saw that Dylan was on the floor, looking at something with a worried expression on his face and the twins were both crying.

"What is it? What's wrong?" Nate asked.

"We found something," Cynthia said, pointing to the floor where Dylan was. Cynthia was obviously trying her best not to let out a sob.

I quickly ran to where Dylan was, and gasped in surprise. Bile rose in my throat and I tried not to throw up. The twins were right, they had found something.

They had found a puddle; a puddle of blood.

ELEVEN

Blood. Red, crimson blood. Looking at it, I wanted to scream. The previous talk with Nate had completely vanished from my mind. All I could think about was the blood. Was it Maya's? What if it was Maya's? What if she had gotten injured?

"It's dry, but it looks fresh," Dylan said, his voice trembling slightly.

It was fresh! That meant that it could have happened only a little while ago. Maya had disappeared about five hours ago, which was not too long. This couldn't be an animal's blood. Or maybe it was. Maybe an animal had gotten injured or killed by a predator. Yeah, that was probably what had happened.

"It's probably just from an injured animal," I said, trying to calm everyone, including myself.

"Something tells me that it's not," Cynthia said, breathing deeply.

I also had that feeling but I was trying to stay positive. I was wanted to comfort myself. Who could have done this? Was it Maya's blood? I felt that there was a connection with the blood and Maya's disappearance.

Dylan and Nate looked at each other. Looking at them, I felt that they knew more than they were letting on. I pulled Dylan aside to ask him.

"You know something about this." It wasn't a question, it was a statement.

Dylan nodded. I waited a second for him to speak, but he only looked back at Nate then met my eyes and shrugged.

"Are you going to tell me?" I exclaimed, irritated.

Dylan bit his lip and looked away. I was really getting worried, he never acted this way. He grabbed my hand and pulled me away from everyone so that they couldn't hear what we were saying.

"It's her father." That was all he said. He was so irritating! Couldn't he elaborate? And what did this have to do with Nate?

"Okay! What about Nate?"

"Umm, no, not Nate. Her real father. Kevin," he said, spitting out the name 'Kevin' as if it was acid on his tongue.

What? Maya knew her father? How was that possible? I had actually forgotten that she was adopted. What would 'Kevin' do? Why would he have something to do with this?

"You mean that Maya knows her parents? And what did her dad do?" I questioned, still in shock.

"Yes, Maya knows her father, not parents. Her mother died. And I'll explain what her father has to do with this, but just one thing, don't call him her 'dad' because she hates that. He's not a 'dad' to her at all." Dylan tensed as he explained all this.

Wow! Her mother was dead. That was sad. What if my parents were dead? I should really go talk to Nate. I shook my head to clear my thoughts. First we had to find Maya.

"Okay, what I'm about to tell you will be a lot to take in, so be ready," Dylan started, looking at me as if asking; 'are you ready to hear what I'm going to say?'.

I nodded, though I was getting nervous about what he was going to say now that he'd taken that tone.

"Fine but you have to promise not to tell Cynthia, Leah, Rana, or Mark. None of them know. They wouldn't be able to handle it," he explained, waiting for me to promise.

"Yes, I promise."

Dylan seemed to reconsider whether he should tell me or not, probably because my voice was shaking. Or he was scared that I would tell Rana, Mark, or one of the twins, or he thought that I wouldn't be able to handle what he was going to say. It couldn't be that bad, right?

"Okay." Dylan took a deep breath, bracing himself for my reaction. "Maya's father has done this once before. I'm going to start from the beginning. Maya's mom got pregnant a few years after she and Kevin had gotten married. Kevin never wanted a child because he thought that it would be too much to deal with, both financially and physically." Dylan paused and looked over my shoulder.

"Maya's mother died while giving birth to Maya. When she died Kevin blamed it on Maya and left her at an orphanage. He showed up three times in the past five years, wanting us to give him money as compensation for his wife's death. The first time he came we were all shocked. He asked us for the money. The second time, he once again asked for money. And the last time, he threatened to take Maya and keep her till we paid. All those times the younger kids were asleep or in their room, so that's why they don't know about it. We never told the police because Maya told us not to. I don't understand why for sure, but I think she feels it's her fault that her mom died. I think she blames herself, and she wants to be punished, however wrong that sounds." He paused again. When I didn't say anything, he continued.

"As you know we don't have that much money, but we have money hidden somewhere in case of an emergency. Somehow, Kevin must know about that money. He wants it. We never thought he would go as far as to actually hold his own daughter for ransom, but we might have just been proven wrong."

Dylan was right; I was completely shocked by what he told me. I closed my eyes and put my hands on Dylan's shoulder for support, feeling suddenly overwhelmed and dizzy. This was so much to take in. My breathing got heavy; this all meant that Maya was probably in the hands of someone really dangerous who would do anything for money, including hurting his own daughter.

We walked back over to the twins.

It had been six hours since Maya's disappearance. After learning about her crazy father, I was scared to death. What had her father done to her? Why was there blood on the ground? Was Maya okay? My breathing came faster and faster until I felt on the verge of collapse. Maya could be in huge danger now. Would Maya's father actually hurt her? Was he the cause of the puddle of blood?

"Dylan, weren't there small drops of blood next to the puddle? Can't we follow them?" I asked, looking at Dylan who was talking to the twins. As I said those words, Dylan's head snapped up and the twins' sad eyes immediately transformed with a faint hint of something that looked like hope.

"There are drops on the ground? Are you serious? How come I didn't see them? " Dylan said in excitement, jumping up and hugging me. Wow! I was not used to seeing Dylan like this. I patted

Dylan's back awkwardly. Dylan pulled back and shouted to Nate, who was on the phone talking to Anne, pacing a few yards deeper into the trees.

Seeing Dylan's expression, Nate jogged closer, dropping the call, concern written on his face. "What is it?" he asked with a hint of desperation in his voices.

"Dad, calm down.." Nate's tense shoulders relaxed slightly. "Ashley noticed that there were drops of blood and realized that we could follow them!" Dylan finished excitedly.

"Yes!" Nate said so loudly that I thought my eardrums would burst. "Duh!" He ran to the blood and immediately started following the trail.

"Dad wait. I'm coming with you!" Dylan called after his dad.

Nate stopped in his tracks and turned to us. "No, you can't come, it might be dangerous."

The twins' faces twisted into confusion. "What do you mean dangerous? Maya might have gotten hurt and walked some place, but it can't be dangerous, can it? There are no wolves or tigers or anything…" Leah trailed off, oblivious to Maya's real father.

Nate faced the twins nervously. Oh no! What was he going to say? He couldn't tell them the truth, but he couldn't lie either, could he?

"No, umm, I meant dangerous in case, umm, she, uh yeah, you know what?" He quickly changed the subject. "Why don't you girls go tell your mom about what we're doing? Ashley could you go with them?" Wait, did he just ask me to go with the twins instead of searching for Maya? Was he completely out of his mind?

"No, the twins can go by themselves. I want to look for Maya too," I declared, standing my ground.

"Ashley, please go with the twins. They can't go by themselves!"

"Uh, excuse me, why?" I put my hands on my hips. "Why can't they go by themselves? They won't get lost or anything. They've lived here their whole lives, I think, and I've just been here for a short while. And anyways, I have the right to go with you."

Nate sighed as he realized that I wouldn't budge.

"And besides, when did sisters start listening to their brothers?" I muttered, causing Nate to smile.

"Okay, you girls go by yourselves. Ashley, Dylan, and I will search for Maya." Nate frowned as he said this, obviously peeved at being bested.

"No Dad, we want to search for Maya too," Cynthia whined.

"I am your father, and you will do as I say. Go tell your mom about Ashley's idea." Nate declared with authority.

The girls sighed and turned away, dragging their feet towards the house.

"Party pooper." One of them muttered.

"Okay guys," Nate said and clapped his hands determinedly. "Let's search. We'll follow the trail of blood and see where it leads."

We walked for what seemed like hours before the blood suddenly stopped. When the drops of blood weren't there anymore, we could see faint hints of footsteps in an area where the soil was softer than it had been before, and we followed that. The footsteps stopped at the foot of a low hill blocking our view of the horizon. We slowly scrambled up the hill, scattering dirt, and abruptly stopped at the top. A small house came into view just beyond the hill, in its shadow, nestled between the hill and the trees. The house was made of stone and it had a wooden door. Quaint and quite small. It probably had four rooms at most.

"Wow!" Dylan said, clearly surprised. "Has he been living here this whole time without us even knowing?"

"Shh! Be quiet!" Nate whisper-shouted. "He might hear us!"

So Maya had a mean father who had just kidnapped her. He most likely lived in a log cabin in the woods only a few hours from Nate's house. He wanted money. This was too much for me to handle! For some reason I felt frustrated and a tear sprang to my eye. Maybe it was because Maya had become as close as a sister to me in these few days I had gotten to know her. I was scared that she was hurt badly. I suddenly felt the urge to scream. Blinking a few times, I told myself to calm down and to think rationally.

"Guys, just wondering, isn't it a bit weird that there was a trail of blood leading us to footsteps, leading us to the place we were looking for? Doesn't it seem planned out?" I asked, curious to see if anyone had had the same thoughts as me.

"That's also what I was thinking, but why would Kevin want us to find him?" Dylan said.

"Right. You're right. Sorry, I'm just kind of scared." I shook my head and breathed deeply.

"Don't worry, we're all freaked out here." Nate said and placed a hand on my shoulder.

"Okay, how are we going to get Maya?" I asked nervously.

"If we want to get her out of there," Dylan started, "then we'll need a plan."

TWELVE

Dylan's plan was, to put it mildly, extreme. I didn't know if we would be able to do what he had in mind without getting caught. We weren't in some kind of movie or book where all the characters lived happily ever after. If Maya's father was dangerous, we could die with this plan –that is, if we got caught.

Even though this plan was dangerous, I would do this for my niece, for my friend. I would do anything for her. In the short time that I had known her, I had come to love her. She supported me and brought me joy, and even though I had known her for less than a week, she was my best friend.

I took a deep breath, bracing myself for what we were about to do. A rush of excitement coursed through my veins; even though this wasn't safe, I lived for adventure. This was the type of thing that only happened in movies, so it was pretty exciting—even with the threat of death looming over us. Wow, I really needed to calm down. My thoughts were so jumbled.

"Okay guys, are you ready?" I asked nervously. I really didn't get myself; one second I was excited, the next I was nervous. The guys both nodded their heads. Before I could talk myself out of it, I raced down the hill. My heart was beating so hard that I thought it would jump out of my chest at any second. What if Kevin—Maya's father—saw me as I was running down the hill? I forced my legs to run faster as I neared the house. When I finally reached the house, I went around its side, pressed my back against the wall, and looking up at the small window above me. I tried to stay quiet, but I was panting heavily from the sprint down the hill.

When I finally caught my breath, I signaled for Nate to come down. When Nate got to where I was, I gestured for him to bend down on the floor like we had talked about in our plan. As he dropped to his hands and knees on the ground, right under the window, I let out a nervous breath before standing on his back and putting both my hands on the window, pushing gently. The window creaked slightly as it opened.

It opened! That was what we had hoped for. If it had been locked, the whole plan would have been ruined. Putting my hands on the windowpane outside, careful not to push the flowers by mistake, I pulled myself up with little effort. The reason that I was the one going inside the house was because I was the only one who could fit through the small window.

I put one knee on the windowpane, praying that it wouldn't break. It looked strong enough. I put my other knee on it. Luckily, it held. Grimacing slightly, I put both my hands on each side of the window, lifted my legs inside the room—whatever room it was— and sat down on the window's edge. I jumped inside the room and neatly landed on my feet.

Scanning the room, I noticed that it was very plain; it only consisted of a small bed and a closet. That was it. The closet was a black color and the bed sheet was also black. The paint on the walls was chipped and faded. I burst out laughing as I thought of the flowers outside his window. Flowers were a sign of beauty and purity. It was as though Kevin was trying to disguise himself as an innocent guy, while in reality, he was—as was his whole room—

dark and menacing. He was not so innocent. That reminded me of the reason I was here and I immediately sobered up. I really was an idiot. Here I was, laughing, while I could have easily gotten caught. Luckily though, it didn't seem as though whoever was in this house had heard me.

I quietly walked to the door, pressing my back right next to its frame. I peeked out of the door, thankfully not seeing anyone in the long hallway. Stepping out of the room, I tried my best to remain silent. As I had previously predicted, there were only four rooms in the house, as I could see only five doors. The fifth door was probably the entrance. I stuck my head in the first room. It was only the bathroom. I peeked into the second room and almost gasped in surprise before closing my eyes.

Taking a few deep breaths, I changed my expression from one of pure fear into one of determination. I looked again. An awful man sat at a table, his yellowed fingernails picking at his food. His grey blue eyes where glassy and empty, cruel almost, yet they held some strange gravity to them, as if they would drag you in. His thin lips where curved in a severe grimace and his dark greasy hair fell in an unkempt way in front of his eyes, as if giving me a brief reprieve from their stare.

Flattening my back against the wall, I looked away from the awful man. His eyes held such darkness that it made him look completely evil. Maya's eyes were the same color and shape as his, but hers were filled with kindness and compassion. Just looking at this mans eyes paralyzed me with fear. My heart started hammering thunderously inside my chest and I felt a trickle of sweat slowly dripping from my forehead. I shook my head. I was here for Maya, not to think about how creepy this man was.

I tiptoed to the next door and saw that it was a small TV room. I quietly went to the door across from it, hoping that I wouldn't get caught. This door was closed, unlike the other doors in this creepy house. Slowly opening it, I prayed that it wouldn't creak. My eyes widened and I gasped.

Maya was tied to a chair, her beautiful eyes were swollen and scrunched nearly shut. Her cheeks where red and had puffy hand prints on them. Silver duct tape sealed her mouth shut and when her eyes met mine she began rocking in the chair and her mouth was frantically working to rid itself of its bindings.

I ran to her, stumbling over my own feet, before I reached the chair. I knelt down in front of her and gently swept away some of the tears falling from her eyes. I slowly started to take away the tape, not wanting to hurt her. As soon as the tape was gone, she started talking to me.

"What are you doing here?" she fervently whispered. "Do you know how dangerous it is? I want you to leave right now! I'll be okay, I promise! Just leave, please." Her tone was urgent, her voice raw. The fact that she was worried about me when she was the one tied up to the chair made me want to cry.

"It'll be okay, Maya. I came here to help you get away. Don't worry, it'll be okay. I promise," I whispered, gently stroking her hair, before I started working on getting her hands free. My frustration built as I struggled and wrestled with the tightly bound and knotted ropes. It was impossible. I grit my teeth and held back further tears.

My teeth! I tried breaking it with my teeth, but to no avail. The grittiness of it just made me nauseous. Just as I was about to give up, I felt something brush against my leg and I remembered that I had a pocket knife in my pocket. Taking it out, I started cutting the thick hay-colored chords of rope. Maya just stared at me in admiration, her face red and white. Just as I was about to finish cutting the rope off her right hand, a bone chilling voice echoed through the room.

"Well, well, well. What have we got here?"

THIRTEEN

I squeezed my eyes shut and stopped breathing, hoping that I would somehow disappear. It obviously didn't work. My heart was beating so hard that I thought it would leap out of my chest any second now. The man was behind me! That evil, wicked man was right behind me. Maybe I could run past him and escape through the window. What if he caught me before I could run past him? I looked at Maya hoping that she had some sort of plan.

As I looked at her face, I suddenly felt very selfish. Her eyes had widened and she was biting her bottom lip so hard that it had turned white. Her eyes had emptied and looked almost lifeless. She had worry lines on her forehead, making her look older than she was. As I stared into her empty eyes I saw a flash of fear cross through them. I was worrying about this man hurting me, while I should have been worrying about Maya. I was really an awful friend.

The voice talked again, snapping me out of my thoughts. "Did ya really think that ya could save her?" He spat the word 'save' out as if it was poison on his tongue. "Ya think I'm a complete idiot? I ain't. Did ya think that I didn't know what was goin' on?"

He then laughed. I shuddered. That sound was a sound I would never forget. A rasping, grating, shiver-inducing laugh filled with venom and hate, like a snake's hiss. His laugh was one of the many things that proved that he was, in fact, evil.

I forced myself to turn around, to be brave. Although I had already seen what he looked like, seeing him again almost made me gasp in horror. His thin lips were twisted into an atrocious smile. His mean eyes stared right back at my green ones. His greasy hair almost completely covered one of his eyes, making him seem even more menacing, if that was possible.

I looked at Maya again and saw that tears were beginning to form in her eyes. I felt a pang in my heart. Maybe when I had come to save her, she had hoped that we would escape. Now looking at her, I knew all her hope was gone.

"Please," she whispered, "Please, don't hurt her. You want me, not her." Although she was weak and she was crying, she sounded brave. Her words hit me like freezing water.

"No!" I yelled before I could stop myself. "No! Please let Maya go. We'll give you the money. Anything, just please, let her come with me." My eyes pleading, I stared at the man, wishing—hoping—that he would let Maya leave.

"Unfortunately honey, I ain't able to do that." His voice was low and scratchy. "Ya know now where I live, and you could call the cops on me. I don't wanna go to jail again, no sir."

I hadn't even thought about that; about the fact that we could call the police. Maybe Nate and Dylan would think of it. That thought gave me hope. Maybe we would be able to escape after all! I then remembered that Nate lived in the middle of nowhere. A thought hit me; it was as though he didn't want to be found.

A big, hairy hand slammed on my shoulder, making me jump in surprise. I looked up and saw the man—Kevin—staring at me.

"Now we don't want ya blabberin' to the cops, ay honey?" Would he stop calling me honey? It was really creepy.

Before I could process what was happening I was slammed into a wall. Pain surged through my cheek as it hit the cold surface. My knees buckled slightly in pain. Both my wrists were gripped tightly behind my back, strong hands holding them firmly.

"No!" I heard Maya yell. A sob escaped her lips and I could hear her sniffing. "Please"—her voice cracked—"Please don't hurt her." Although I couldn't see her from my position, I imagined her looking at her father.

"Quit your yappin' unless you want me to hurt 'er more," Kevin barked at his daughter. I felt a rope being looped and tugged tight around my wrists, too tight for comfort, scratching my skin and squeezing my pulse. Kevin kicked my leg and I toppled to the ground, unable to save face with my hands tied. Pain burst from my nose and I felt something wet trickling down between my nose and mouth.

Again I felt a rope being tightly bound around my ankles. I tried to turn my head but I couldn't. Kevin's face appeared in front of me.

"Ya won't be able to go blabber to the cops now, will ya?" He turned away from me and I heard him walk towards Maya. He was probably going to tie her up again. After what seemed like hours, I finally heard an uneven beat of footsteps, starting out loud but slowly fading away. He was gone.

"Maya! Are you okay?" My voice was laced in worry as I tried to look at Maya, my cheek still pressed to the carpet.

"I've never been better." Her voice was strained and weak. "Are you okay? I'm so sorry for dragging you into this mess. I'm so sorry for not telling you about my father. Please forgive me. I'm sorry for being the cause of you coming here. I'm really sorry. You shouldn't have come! Kevin is dangerous. He can hurt you. You shouldn't have come to save me. And now you're here because of me. I'm sorry..." Her voice trailed off in a whisper as I heard soft sounds of sniffling. She was crying.

"Maya, calm down. It's okay. Don't worry about me. Worry about yourself. Please don't cry Maya." I wished I could go to her and hug her, comfort her. But I couldn't because I was tied up. We both couldn't move. We both couldn't escape.

The ropes were cutting at my wrists, they were probably going to leave marks. Maya was sniffling lightly. We had been in this place for about an hour I would say. The cold was starting to seep into me from the floor.

I wondered what Dylan and Nate were doing. Had they called the police yet? Had they gone back home to get help? Would one of them climb in to try and rescue us? Would they really do that? I didn't know. I couldn't think straight. I tried not to close my eyes because every time I closed my eyes I saw a picture of Kevin's face. I wished I hadn't followed the trail of blood. That thought popped out of nowhere, making me feel guilty. Maya was the one that had caused that trail of blood. She was the one that had gotten hurt, not me.

Maya. Cut. Blood. My head jerked back to look at Maya as I

thought of this. I hadn't seen a gash and I had completely forgotten that Maya was probably the one that had caused the trail of blood.

"Maya, did you get hurt? Are you the one that caused the trail of blood? Did Kevin hurt you?" Maya's sniffles got louder.

"Yes, he did it. He cut the top of my arm, but barely. He wanted you to find me. He did it on purpose. He knew you would see it and he knew you would follow it. He wanted to get one more person to hold as ransom so that Dad would have no choice but to pay the money." At first I was confused as to what she meant by "dad". Kevin? No, she must have meant Nate. I remembered what Dylan had said and bit my lip.

Having time to process what had just happened, I gasped in horror. How could someone do that? How could someone be so evil as to actually hurt his own daughter just to have one more person to tie up in a room? All of that just for money? It was too confusing.

I squeezed my eyes shut, hoping that would help me concentrate. The sound of footsteps caused me to open my eyes. The footsteps grew louder as the person came closer. With these footsteps, I felt some hope light up inside me. Had Nate or Dylan come to rescue us? And then fear twisted my gut. Or was Kevin coming back to hurt us?

My worst fears were confirmed when Kevin's face appeared through the opening sliver of light from the door. His eyes roamed the place, as if he was trying to see if we had done any damage. As if we could do damage. We were tied up, for heaven's sake!

"Well I see your little friends didn't come to save ya, huh?" His lips curved up into an ugly grimace. "I guess they think you're not worth payin' money for. Ya ain't valuable enough. I gotta get someone more valuable. How about that tiny girl? The one that can't even speak right. You're so worthless that even your friends don't wanna pay money to free ya. Ain't that funny?"

A surge of anger burst through me. He wanted to take Rana.

"We're not worthless. How dare you speak to us like that! And would you stop calling them our little friends? They're our family! They're coming for us! You wait and see. You'll never be able to get Rana." I spat out.

I soon regretted my words as Kevin's face transformed into one of anger. He took two long, slow strides towards me, stopping right in front of my face. I felt a burst of pain in my stomach as Kevin's foot slammed into it. I cried out. He wore heavy-duty boots that felt like bricks when they slammed into my body. Nausea bloomed with a deep ache in my stomach.

"Ya never, ever, talk to me like that again. Ya got it?" He paused and looked down at me. I quickly nodded, fearing that he would hurt me again, tears running from my eyes. "Good." With that last word, he walked out of the room, shutting the door on his way out.

As soon as he was gone, I let out a cry of pain, trying to clutch my stomach. Of course, I wasn't able to, but I curled into a fetal position to try to stop the ache.

"Are you okay? Please be okay! I'm so sorry. This is all my fault!" Maya started crying again.

"Maya, stop crying. I'm okay, I promise. It's not your fault. Please calm down," I said in a soft voice, wincing slightly at the pain in my stomach. A few minutes passed in silence before I heard the sound of footsteps again.

The door slowly creaked open and I looked up, thinking that I would see Kevin.

Instead, I saw Dylan.

FOURTEEN

Dylan was here! I blinked hard a few times, thinking I was dreaming.

Dylan gasped when he saw Maya. He turned to me and gasped again.

"Dylan!" I whisper-growled. "Dylan, come! Quick! Be careful! Kevin's still here!" Dylan seemed paralyzed with fear, just gaping at us. He shook his head quickly.

"Don't worry, I saw him leave the house. That's why I came in." My shoulders sagged with relief. Kevin was gone. Dylan was here. We would escape. Tears started to form in my eyes but I blinked them away.

Dylan rushed to Maya, looking around for something to cut off the ropes. My pocketknife! Where had Kevin put it? I looked around, searching for it. When I didn't see it, I felt stupid. As if Kevin would be dumb enough to leave my pocketknife in the room Maya and I were in. Maybe he'd left it in his room.

"Dylan, look in Kevin's room! He took my pocketknife and hopefully he left it there."

Dylan glanced at me before running out of the room. He came back a few minutes later, holding my pocketknife.

"You'd think that he would be smarter." Dylan tsked. "I found it on his bed." Despite myself, I cracked a smile.

Dylan rushed over to Maya and started cutting the ropes tied to her wrists. When he was done, he went to her ankles. As soon as Maya was free, she jumped up and wrapped her arms around Dylan.

"Thank you so much," she said, letting her tears flow freely. Dylan hugged her back and looked like he might start crying too.

"Guys this is very sentimental and cute, but I'm still tied up here!"

Dylan untangled himself from Maya's embrace and jogged to me.

"Sorry," he said sheepishly and started cutting at the ropes around my wrists. I just rolled my eyes at him, suddenly feeling at ease again. Everything was going to be okay. After a few minutes of Dylan's rope hacking, I was free. I jumped to my feet and thanked Dylan with a big hug, but groaned at the pain in my stomach. It hadn't gone away. Along with the external pain of Kevin's kick, I felt an internal pain; a twist in my gut telling me that something was wrong.

"Come on! Let's hurry up!" Although Dylan said that Kevin had left the house, I knew that he could come back at any second. Maya and Dylan nodded and rushed out of the room, with me following close behind them. We soon arrived at the front door.

"I think it would be safer if we looked first," Maya said cautiously. I nodded and went closer to the door. I opened it slightly and looked through it. When I saw that the coast was clear, I gave Dylan and Maya a thumbs up.

I opened the door fully and allowed them to exit. I followed them and quietly closed the door behind me. Turning around, I saw that Maya and Dylan were already half way up the hill. As I ran after them, I stumbled a little, my muscles cold and aching, but I quickly caught myself and continued running, trying to ignore the stab in my stomach.

Maya and Dylan had already reached the other side of the hill when I reached them. I was relieved to see that Nate, Josh, and the twins, were there, waiting for us. The twins were hugging Maya and they looked relieved, mortified, and angry at the same time.

"How could you keep this from us?" Leah asked, Maya looked surprised for a second but Cynthia stopped any question Maya was about to ask. "Nate told us. You should have told us, you know! We're your sisters after all."

As they spoke, Maya's eyes turned glassy. I guess that after being taken by her father it felt good to know that she still had some family who loved her. Nate and Josh walked up to Maya, taking turns hugging her. I just watched awkwardly, not wanting to interrupt their family moment, my arms wrapped around my stomach. It helped a bit, but I still felt nauseous and unreasonably afraid.

Josh must have seen that I was feeling a little left out so he came over to me and hugged me. "I'm so happy you're okay! I was so worried for my favorite aunt." I blushed a little and hugged him back.

"Us too!" The twins said at the same time. Again, creepy. Nate came to me and squeezed me as if his life depended on it. Ouch! I kept the yell of pain inside and bit my lip.

"I was so worried. I'm so happy that you're okay! Did he hurt you? Are you feeling fine? Do you feel sick?" Nate asked, concerned. I wasn't used to this. Having so much affection and care directed towards me made me feel loved and special.

I squeezed my eyes shut, not wanting to start crying now. A tear escaped anyways.

Even though everything that had happened seemed bad, things would be okay now. Even though I had been tied up and kicked, everything would be okay. Even though Kevin had threatened me, everything would be okay. Even though Kevin said that he would take Rana because I wasn't valuable enough, everything would be— Rana! He left to take Rana!

FIFTEEN

When the thought—Kevin went to take Rana—hit me, I stopped moving and breathing. I felt a pang in my heart near as painful as the throb in my stomach. Everything seemed to be tilting. He went to take my niece. Suddenly, I turned, angry. I felt heat burn on my cheeks with my fury. Who did the man think he was?

"Ashley? Ash, you okay?" Nate asked, concerned. His face was wrinkled with worry and I realized that he had been calling me for a while. The twins, Josh, and Dylan also looked concerned but Maya's face was squished in confusion, as if she was trying to piece a puzzle together. Her face suddenly relaxed in realization and she looked directly at me. She knew what I was thinking. She squeezed her eyes shut and it seemed as though she would start crying again.

"Girls, what's going on?" Nate asked.

We had to do something! We had to get back to Nate's house before something happened to Rana; before Kevin took her.

"Kevin went to take Rana."

With those five simple words from Maya, Leah burst into tears and Nate turned pale. Cynthia's jaw had fallen open, as if she was waiting for someone to feed her. Josh's eyes had widened so much that it looked like his eyes would pop out at any second. I looked at Dylan and saw that he understood what I was thinking; we had to act now, we had to get home. No time for crying.

"Everyone, get it together. Crying and wailing won't do us any good. Let's go." Dylan's voice held so much authority and power that I almost took a step back. He was right though, we had to go.

Leah stopped crying and Cynthia closed her mouth. They knew we were right. I broke into a run and headed towards Nate's house, not looking to see if the others were following me, biting against the ache that still hadn't disappeared.

I got a little confused and lost a few times, not knowing where I was supposed to go, but I just waited for Dylan to run in front of me so that I could follow him. The ache started to dull, but the feeling of wrongness lingered. My imagination circled around dark thoughts. I imagined Rana hurt, screaming, crying and I imagined Kevin with that evil laugh. It drove me to push harder, to run faster. Dylan seemed to have a great sense of direction, because the trail of blood was gone and he looked like he knew exactly where he was going.

I thought about many things as I ran; where Kevin and Rana where at this moment, if Anne, Kyle, and Mark were with Rana, and if they were hurt. I thought about how cruel Kevin was and about how Maya must feel.

What I thought about the most though, was that I still barely knew anything about my past. When I thought about Kevin, I wondered if my dad had been mean. I wondered what had happened to my family to make them leave me. Had I also somehow made my father angry to the point that he didn't want me anymore? Or had I made my mother angry?

Although it seemed like I had been captured for weeks, it had only been a few hours. However, in that short period of time I'd gotten to think a lot.

As I ran and thought, I decided something; I wanted to know

about my past. I had been too easy on Nate, not asking him many questions about my past in case they brought back bad memories for him. Now I'd had enough of that. It was also my past and I had the right to know. I would make him tell me. I would take him aside from the others and demand to know the truth. I snapped out of my thoughts when I realized that we had arrived. Blinking a few times to clear my head, I saw that Nate wanted to open the door and get to Rana. Just as I was about to tell him not to, Josh stopped him.

"We can't do that," Josh whispered harshly. "We need to go in slowly and quietly." Josh was right, if Kevin was still in there, he couldn't know that we were here.

Cynthia quietly opened the door, and I prayed that it wouldn't squeak. Luckily, it didn't. We all tiptoed into the house, hoping that the wood wouldn't creak. Everything was going well until I heard a high pitched scream. We all snapped our heads toward the kitchen, which was where the scream had come from. I closed my eyes and exhaled heavily before I began walking towards the kitchen, hoping that Rana was okay.

I would never forget the scene in front of me.

Rana was wailing, her tiny arms wrapped around the arm of a chair. Kevin had both of her legs firmly in his grip and he was trying to pull her off the chair. What hit me the most though, was Rana's face. Her eyes were open wide and her small mouth was pulled into a grimace as she let out panicked screams. I saw a variety of emotions cross her eyes as she cried; fear, terror, surprise, but the one that surprised me most was the glimpse of hatred.

She was too young to hate someone –to even understand what hate was. At that moment, I knew that Rana would remember this day for the rest of her life. Although Kevin wasn't physically hurting her, she was young; she didn't really understand what was going on. All she knew was that some man she'd never seen before was trying to take her away from her house.

Before I could think, I rushed to Kevin and did something I never thought I would do; I punched him in the face. Kevin dropped Rana in surprise, causing her to drop the chair and fall to the floor.

Kevin placed both his hands over his eyes, right where I had punched him. He slowly turned to me. His mouth was slightly parted and his good eye was squinting at me in hatred. I was surprised by what I had done, but I didn't regret it.

One of Kevin hands went off his eyes and flew to my face, punching me on my right cheek. I stumbled back in pain and clutched my cheek with my hands. Kevin gripped my hair and pulled it backwards, forcing me to look at him.

"Don't ya ever do that again. Think I'm a punching bag? Who d'ya think ya are?"

That did it. Who did I think I was? Who did he think he was? I'm treating him like a punching bag? He was treating his own daughter like dirt. I gripped his hand that was tightly grasping my hair and pulled it away. I took his hand in a full grip and pushed him back forcefully. My push was so hard that he hit the wall. His face contorted in pain and as he pushed himself off the wall, he lunged at me.

Before he could touch me though, Josh, Dylan, and Nate –who had been by the door, too shocked to move—had Kevin pinned against the wall. Nate was holding Kevin's right arm against the wall and Josh was holding Kevin's left arm against the wall, while Dylan pushed against both of Kevin's shoulders. Kevin tried to get out from their grasps, but even though he was very muscular, the fact that they were three kept him in his place.

"What do we do?" I asked, panicked. We couldn't call the cops, could we? They would know where Nate and his family lived and that wouldn't be good. Come to think of it, why wouldn't that be good? Why does Nate live so far away from civilization? No, this was not the time to think of such things.

"There's only one thing to do," Nate started, "we have to call the cops." I raised my eyebrows at Josh. Nate wanted to call the cops? Well, I guess he was right; there was nothing else to do.

"Josh, you and Dylan are going to go out of the woods with this man and hand him over to the police. We'll tell them to meet you by the pond near the entrance of the woods. Now go, and I'll give you a gun just in case." The boys nodded. Nate was furious and it showed in the way he growled his words.

"What! No! I can't go to jail again! Leave me alone!" Kevin struggled under their firm grasps, then he looked directly at Maya. "This is your fault! Your fault, you murderer! You killed my wife! Murderer!"

Before I could register his words, Nate's left fist hit Kevin right in the eye—his good eye—before his right fist connected with Kevin's jaw.

"Don't you dare talk to my daughter like that! Do you hear me? And don't you dare come back here. If I ever see your face again, you'll be sorry." Nate bared his teeth and shook his hand. He looked madder than I'd ever seen him. Nate turned to Dylan and Josh. "I'll go get the gun, boys. Hold him well."

Dylan and Josh nodded as Nate disappeared. Nate arrived a few minutes later, holding a big, long gun. He seemed to have calmed down a little.

"I called the cops and told them to meet you guys near the pond right after the entrance of the woods. I told them that he was stealing from our house." Nate gestured at Kevin with his head, before handing the gun he was holding to Dylan. "If he tries anything, shoot his leg."

With that, the boys left, and Nate walked over to me.

"Are you okay? Did he hurt you?" Nate asked. I quickly shook my head. My face didn't hurt that much and the ache in my middle had dwindled to a constant stinging sensation I could ignore. Nate nodded and went over to Rana, asking her the same question. Rana burst into tears and Nate hugged her.

"What happened, Rana?" Nate asked. "Where's mom? And where are Mark and Kyle?"

"Mommy went outside to wook fow you. Mawk and Kywle went to Kywle's room to pway video games becauth Kywle sawd he wath stew- stws- stwethed." Rana spoke in words interrupted by tears and sniffling into Nate's shoulder. I would have smiled at how she had tried to say 'stressed' if we hadn't been in such dire straits.

Nate bit his lower lip in anger and wrapped his arms tightly around Rana before carrying her out of the room. When they were gone, I realized that Maya was staring at me sadly.

"Maya, are you okay? What's wrong?" I know, stupid question. I bet everything was wrong for Maya.

"I'm so sorry for dragging you into this! Please forgive me! I should have told you earlier!" she said, bursting into tears. "Ashley, he called me a murderer. I'm a murderer."

I walked over to Maya, giving her a hug and stroking her hair lightly. "Don't worry Maya, it's fine. You are not a murderer. Maya, you're safe now. Don't worry, you're safe now," I told her, as I felt hope surge through me.

Dylan and Josh arrived half an hour later, assuring us that everything was fine and that they hadn't needed to shoot Kevin's leg or arm. The police had taken Kevin and he was going to get in big trouble because his name was already on the records.

Anne had arrived and she was putting Rana down for a nap. Nate was yelling at Kyle and Mark for leaving Rana alone, his shouts ringing through the whole house. Apparently they hadn't heard the screaming because they had had headphones on. Maya was sitting in a chair, staring into empty space with dead eyes, while I was on the sofa, biting my nails and trying to ignore that feeling of wrongness.

We were all shaken, but I knew we would be fine eventually.

I snapped my head towards the stairs when I heard a ring of footsteps. First, Nate came down, followed by Kyle and Mark, who both wore sheepish expressions.

"I—I know that these few days has been very hard for all of you," Nate said. He paused to look at each one of us in the eyes. "And I know that we will never forget these few days, but it, umm, it made us all stronger, I guess. The thing that you all need to know though, is that we're fine now. Kevin is gone and we'll be fine... Why don't we all rest for a while? We deserve some sleep."

When his eyes met mine, I shook my head. I wanted him to understand that I needed answers. Nate sighed as if he had expected that.

"Everyone go and rest," Nate said again. "Ashley, stay here."

No one argued, they all just nodded and went towards their rooms. Everyone was too tired to refuse.

Nate slowly walked over to me, taking my hand and pulling me towards his office. He opened the door and walked into the room. He sat behind his desk and gestured for me to sit in a chair. I sat in a slightly torn chair and turned it to face Nate. He cleared his throat.

"You wanted to talk to me?" he asked nervously. He started tapping his finger against the table, making a little beat. His eyes wouldn't meet mine, as if he was scared of what I would ask him.

"Yeah...I, umm, I was thinking about everything that happened. About Maya's father and all that. Well, umm, it made me think of my—our—parents, and why they left me at an orphanage, if they also had something against me." I paused to look at Nate. He was biting his lip and his hands were knotted together.

"I, uh, I want to know about my past. I don't want to be left in the dark anymore. I need to know. They were also my parents. I know you're tired with everything that's happened in the past few days, so maybe you can tell me a little now and the rest tomorrow. But I want to know." My hand twitched nervously as I finished.

I kept my eyes trained on the carved wood of the desk as I waited for Nate to speak. "I know. You deserve to know," Nate finally said with a sigh. I looked up at him, surprised. I thought that I would have to put up a fight. I guess Nate understood how important this was to me.

"Why don't I start telling you about our parents? How they were. Tomorrow I'll tell you the rest." He looked at me questioningly and I nodded my agreement. "Our mom's name was Sandra and our dad's name was John." I nodded my head in recognition; Josh had mentioned that the first time we met, but then my head tilted slightly as I replayed what Nate had said. He said 'was' not 'is'. Why had he said that? Were our parents dead?

Nate must have seen that I was about to ask that question, because he shook his head. "Tomorrow," he said. I nodded again.

"Our mom was a nurse and our dad was a doctor. That's how they met," he said, a small smile playing on his lips. I felt a pang of jealousy that Nate knew our parents. "You had a locket with a picture of Mom and Dad, right? You talked about it when we were walking to your aunt and uncle's house to put that note there." I nodded for what felt like the millionth time.

"So you know what Mom and Dad looked like. Dad was a very funny guy. He was always busy with his work, but he wasn't so busy that he didn't have time for mom and me." Nate glanced at me before continuing. "He loved basketball. He was very good at it. I always admired his throws. He always made the ball go in an arch and enter the net smoothly. I remember when he taught me how to play."

My eyes were shut tight as I took in all that information. My dream had always been to learn a little more about my biological parents, and now that it was happening it felt like a shock one felt after entering cold water. I never thought I would hear about them.

"Mom was the best cook to ever live. Her brownies and cupcakes were excellent and her steaks were the best. I remember once she tried to teach me how to make chocolate-chip cookies, and I almost burned down the kitchen." Nate's face turned distant and angry all of a sudden, and I wondered why.

Nate shook his head and continued telling me about our parents. "Dad always tried to teach mom how to shoot a basket, but she always missed. Her dribbling was horrible." Nate chuckled a little, looking into space, probably remembering.

Suddenly his face turned stony. "I've told you enough for one day. You should go to bed." I started to protest but Nate just shushed me. I bit the inside of my cheeks and walked out of the room, trying to keep in mind that it was probably hard for him to talk about this —about our parents. But I had a right to know. They were also my parents.

I just sighed as I entered the guest room. I changed into the pajamas that Maya had given me and headed to bed, knowing that the next day would be a long one.

SIXTEEN

I felt warm light shining on my face. I cracked my eyes open only to close them again because of the blinding light. Putting a hand in front of my face to shield my eyes, I slowly opened them again. The light was coming from the window; the sun was shining brightly behind the thick glass. Standing up, I stood by the window and looked outside. Despite what had happened in the last few days, I found myself smiling. A few leaves rustled in the air and the flowers danced rhythmically.

I let out a sigh of contentment as I watched the peaceful view. I let myself be hypnotized by the beauty of nature. I left my worries behind as I watched a squirrel lick his whiskers. The squirrel looked so peaceful; not a care in the world. It lived its life day by day, probably not worrying about the next day. Lucky squirrel. I wished I could be like that; not worrying about tomorrow, not worrying about today.

I was so mesmerized by the beauty of the world outside that I barely heard the knock on my door.

"Come in," I said, clearing my throat.

The door slowly creaked open to reveal Maya's face. She had dark circles around her eyes, a sign that she hadn't slept well last night. She walked over to me, sat on the windowsill and looked outside as well. Her lips pulled up into a genuine smile.

We didn't talk. We simply shared a comfortable silence.

Finally, after a long while, Maya cleared her throat. She looked at me and smiled. Maya's blue eyes looked into my green ones. Her eyes looked like an ocean after a storm; they were sharp and clear, red rimmed from lack of sleep and probably from crying.

"I have a few things to tell you," Maya said. "First of all, I want to apologize for what happened. It was my fault." I was about to protest, but Maya lifted up a hand, signaling forr me to stop.

"Please, let me finish," she said, to which I nodded. "It was my fault, because I shouldn't have let my guard down. I should have known that Kevin was serious. I thought it was all just an empty threat. I didn't think he would actually hurt one of us. I was wrong. I'm sorry. Please, try to forget these past few days. I know it'll be hard, but try. And dad is right, it made us stronger. We know the real world now. The real world is dangerous."

She stopped for a second, breathing in and out slowly.

"You're right, Maya. We know the real world now. We know that it's not all rainbows and unicorns. You want to know a famous saying by a guy called J-something?" I asked. Maya nodded. "He said, 'Life without a fight is just a dream.' He was right. In life, we have to fight. We won't always win, but we will progress and we will learn from our mistakes. Let's not think negative." I walked over to Maya and held both her hands in mine.

"And I don't think we should forget about what happened in the past few days. It's important to remember. We learned a lesson from all of this; we learned that there's always a way out. We thought it was hopeless, but we were wrong. We also learned that we can't do everything by ourselves; we need to learn to accept help from other people." I looked Maya straight in the eyes, showing her how serious I was.

"Maya, you need help. You need to be comforted. You need help to be yourself again. I need help too. I need help to not look over my shoulder in fear everywhere I go. We'll help each other. Maya, you know you could have told me about Kevin before this all happened. At least I would have known. You don't need to go against this world alone. I can help you. I know we haven't even known each other for a week, but to me, it seems like a lifetime. You can trust me with anything you need," I finished and hugged Maya.

We stayed like that for a while, just hugging each other, knowing that the other would always be there when we needed them. We finally pulled away.

Maya wiped away a stray tear and looked at me. "There's a second thing I wanted to tell you," she started. I nodded, signaling for her to continue. "In about a week, it's Mark's birthday. He'll be turning eleven. Every birthday in our family, we start a campfire near the house and have hotdogs. Then we roast marshmallows and we make s'mores. It's kind of like a family tradition," she finished, smiling.

"Awesome! So next week, huh? That makes it the twenty-ninth of June?" I asked. I was excited, since I loved my nephew. I would buy him the coolest gift ever! And I also loved s'mores!

Maya shook her head. "No, it's the third of July," she corrected. "When's your birthday?" she asked curiously.

"Thirty-first of August. You?" I asked back, also curious.

"Mine is the twenty-seventh of April," she said, a smile playing on her lips. "Why? Are you already planning out the birthday gift you'll give me?" she asked teasingly.

"Yeah, I was thinking I could give you one of my dirty socks and sew two buttons on it to make you a puppet-sock," I teased back. Maya just laughed lightly and stuck her tongue out at me.

"Mom and Dad are in the living room and they want to tell us something. We should probably go down," she said.

I nodded and followed her out of my room and to the living room.

Nate and Anne were sitting on a couch. Rana was asleep on Anne's lap, Mark was lounging on a rocking chair, and the twins, Josh, Dylan, and Kyle, were sitting on a second couch. Maya and I took a chair from the table in the kitchen and sat next to everyone else.

Everyone was chatting and laughing, like a real family. Maya and I joined in on Mark and Cynthia's conversation. After we had talked for a few minutes, Nate stood up and cleared his throat.

Everyone looked up at him. "Mom and I have an announcement." Nate paused and looked at Anne nervously. "It may surprise you all as it surprised us. We didn't want to tell you too soon, because there was so much going on." Nate took a deep breath. We all waited anxiously for him to tell us the news.

"Your mother is pregnant," he said.

Silence. Thirty seconds of pure silence before the whole room burst into conversation. I just stood there awkwardly, not knowing what to do. Maya was hugging her mom and the twins were excitedly talking, the boys all looked surprised and Rana was still asleep.

I felt like an outsider.

That's when I was hit by a realization. I was going to be the aunt of that baby! I was the baby's aunt! I felt a surge of excitement. I would be there from the baby's first day in the world.

That's when I realized something else. I wanted to stay here. I had finally found my family, and I wasn't leaving. I was going to stay here and watch the new baby grow. I was sure Nate wouldn't mind and I was sure no one else would mind.

I had finally found a home! I finally had a family!

"I win!" I cried in excitement, placing my last Uno card on the deck. Everyone grumbled in annoyance. It was the third time I had won. Tonight was game night again, Rana and Mark were in bed, and Kyle and Nate had gone to buy pizza. They couldn't order a delivery because then the delivery man would have to come here and no one was allowed to see this place.

"Well, you clearly cheated," Josh said.

"Yeah, sure I cheated," I said with a smirk.

"Anyways, as you guys all know, it's Mark's birthday tomorrow," Anne said, getting up and dusting herself off. "So tomorrow night is camp fire night!"

This brought a few whoops from Maya and Leah. Everyone stood up and stretched.

There was a knock at the door, and soon everyone was seated at the large table, eating pizza.

"Okay, so, we bought marshmallows, crackers and chocolate. We also got hotdogs and buns," Nate said in excitement. He was acting like a child who was about to get a candy.

"Yay!" Maya said.

I glanced at Nate, wondering when he was going to talk to me about my parents. He was supposed to tell me a few days ago, but with the excitement of the baby, I didn't want to press him. Nate looked up at me and we staring at each other. *Tomorrow*, Nate seemed to tell me with his eyes.

I sighed. Well, I had waited seventeen years to know the truth, I could wait one more day.

"I have exciting news!" Cynthia suddenly cried out. "I'm going to make an African doll for the new baby!"

Everyone just stared blankly at her.

"Wow, how exciting," Kyle said, his voice dripping sarcasm.

"That's nice, Cynthia, what country?" Leah asked.

"Africa, dummy, I just told you!" Cynthia said, her excitement gone.

"Well, dummy, Africa's a continent, not a country," Leah retorted.

The rest of the night consisted of little fights and arguments, laughter, and smiles.
Today had been a good day, and I wondered what tomorrow would bring. I shook my head. I wasn't going to think about tomorrow; I was going to take it one day at a time and enjoy the little moments.

SEVENTEEN

Today was a day filled with excitement; the camp fire day! Everyone ran around, preparing for tonight. I had gone camping with Andrew and with my adoptive parents, but we had never started a camp fire.

"Ashley!" someone yelled, snapping me out of my thoughts.

"Yes?"

Maya entered my room, jumping up and down. "Do you want to hang out? We still have a few hours to kill before the camp fire." She looked so eager.

I nodded. I loved hanging out with Maya. She was, after all, my best friend.

"Yay! Do you want to go to the secret area?" she asked. I looked at her in confusion. Secret area? What secret area? Then it hit me; the underground place they had showed me before the whole Kevin thing. I had completely forgotten about that.

"Yeah! Let's go there!"

I was holding a bag of chips and some soda as Maya opened the secret door. We jumped inside the underground room and took a seat on the bean-bags after Maya had flicked on the light switch. I opened the bag of chips and offered them to Maya before I tossed her a can of soda.

"Hey Maya, if you don't mind me asking, how do Nate and Anne make money if they don't leave the house?" I had been wondering about that for a while.

"Oh, well they're both authors and they have pen names, so

they're both anonymous." She told me.

Wow, that was cool.

"Anyways, no more boring talk about adult life, let's talk about more interesting things." Maya said. So we did. We stayed in the underground room for what seemed like a life time, just talking about nonsense and enjoying each others' company. I laughed a lot, ate a lot of chips, and didn't spare a thought for what Nate was going to tell me later on in the day. It was great.

Yellow and orange danced and mingled, blurring my vision. The fire warmed me as I sat and stared at it from the log on which I was perched.

Mark was very excited. It *was* his birthday, after all. Once everyone was seated, we roasted sausages to make hotdogs. We all laughed and talked about funny and embarrassing birthday memories. I told them about the time Sara had been jealous that I had gotten a bigger birthday cake than her when I was seven and she "accidentally" flipped the table over, flattening the cake and ruining all the treats stacked on the table. As we laughed, I noticed that Nate looked a little tense and worried, but I let it go. He was a dad and probably felt a bit overprotective about his kids in light of recent events.

When we were done eating hotdogs, we sang "Happy Birthday" to Mark, ate cake, and roasted marshmallows. We were all having a blast. This was one of the best nights of my life. This was how it felt to have a loving family. A tap on my shoulder made me turn around. My heart beat faster when I saw Nate. The nervous look on his face somewhat scared me. Was what he had to say that bad?

"Hey Ash, I need to talk to you," he said.

I stood up and looked at everyone else, but they were busy talking and laughing together, distracted by the fire and the marshmallows and the funny stories. I briefly noticed that Kyle wasn't there, but let it slide; he was probably just taking a walk or something. Maybe he'd gone to the toilet. I walked over to Nate, who took my hand and led me away from everyone else. Nate looked nervously from left to right.

"Nate, what's wrong?" He was really scaring me.

"Look Ash, I think it's time I tell you about our parents."

My heart began to beat even faster, and my palms started to sweat. Did I really want to know this? Did I really want to take the risk of knowing the truth? But I had to know. I needed to know. This was what I wanted, wasn't it?

"Okay, tell me."

"Ash, please don't hate me." Why would I hate him? I was getting dizzy. This could not be good.

"I could never hate you." I told him.

"Okay, so when I was eighteen –I was still living at our house because I was doing a gap year— I made the wrong choices, hung out with the wrong friends. I started doing drugs and other unsavory things. Well, Mom and Dad knew about this, and they wanted me to stop. They tried to make me stop, they really did, but a habit is a habit, and it's hard to stop. Sometimes I would beg them for money so that I could get more drugs but they never gave me any…they thought it would help me stop." Nate took a deep breath in. "One day, I took you to the grocery store. That month, I didn't have enough money to give my drug dealer."

I couldn't breathe. Nate doing drugs? What was this leading to? I felt as though I was going to faint.

"Say it, Nate."

"He was mad. Really mad. He was also drugged and he was an alcoholic. Being mad, drugged, and alcoholic isn't the best combination. He started a fire in our house. He thought that I was in there. Mom and Dad were taking a nap and by the time they woke up it was too late. They were trapped. The dealer got away and was never found." The world spun around me. I couldn't stand anymore so I leaned against a tree.

"Lots of people pitied me and wanted to help, so I got a lot of money and I also inherited all of mom and dad's money. I told the police the name of my drug dealer –the man who had started the fire, but I never told them why he had done what he had done. With the money I had, I decided that I wanted to start a new life, away from everyone I knew. The thing was; I couldn't leave this place. This is where I grew up. So I paid a lot of money for my house to be built and there was just too much going on for me to take care of you."

He paused and looked me in the eye. "I put you up for adoption, and I paid your adoptive parents the money they needed to adopt you, and more. I promised myself that I would find you when you were older. The guilt is still here Ash. I can't stop blaming myself for what happened. It should have been me who had died, not them. I'm so sorry, I really am."

The truth almost knocked me off my feet. He had been half the cause of my parents' death. He had been the cause of the seventeen years of a life without someone who truly loved me other than Andrew. I had always wondered why my biological parents had adopted me —paid so much money to adopt me— if they had never even wanted me. Nate had paid them.

"I, uh, I think I need to take a walk." My limbs trembled and I tried not to look at Nate or meet his eyes. This was too much for me to deal with. "Ye-yeah, that's what I need." I spun on my heel and ran into the darkness, into the woods, and away from him. I ran away from the only true family I had ever known. I ran and ran till I couldn't feel me legs. And then I ran more, until everything was numb and I couldn't feel anything anymore.

EIGHTEEN

The camp fire's light was far behind me and I stumbled through the darkness without any light to guide me. Not caring that I was lost, I ran as if my life depended on it. I didn't know where I was running to, and it didn't matter to me then. I didn't look behind me either. Tears ran freely down my cheeks and my heart ached in my chest. At last, I stumbled over something big and I fell. Even though I help my hands out in front of me, my face still slammed against the dirt. My knees ached and I felt blood start to leak from the wounds. My palms stung too, and my cheek. I put my hand to my face and felt something wet and warm. Blood. What had I tripped over? I felt around on the forest floor until my fingers closed over something cold. I grasped it. Something metal. I pulled on the metal, and I heard a small creak. The secret hideout!

How had I managed to get here? I didn't care, because Nate and Anne didn't know about this place and so there was no way they would find me here, and besides, I really needed some light.

I jumped into the hole and landed on the ground. Shakily I stood up and fumbled around for the light switch. When I found it, I turned the light on. And screamed.

"Kyle?" What was he doing here? I put a shaky hand over my heart.

"Ash! You scared me!" he said.

"I scared you? Really? You scared me! How was I supposed to know you were here? How did you get here in the dark? Why was the light switch turned off? What are you doing here? What—"

"Ashley! Calm down. Breathe. I came here with a flashlight. Ever heard of that? And I turned the light off when I heard a sound outside. I didn't want anyone to find me. And what I'm doing here is none of your business —in fact, I should be asking *you* what you're doing here?"

I hesitated. Should I tell him? Well, I guess that he already knew.

"Um, actually, Nate kind of told me what happened and I kind of ran away, and kind of tripped over the handle to this place's entrance, and I kind of came in." As I spoke, tears started streaming from my eyes again and I swiped at them, feeling stupid. Nate killed my parents. All of it was his fault.

Before I could register what was happening, I felt arms around me. I hugged Kyle back and just cried. I cried till I had no more tears left. I'm not sure how long we stood there, but when my tears had finally run out, Kyle's shirt was soaked around his shoulders. Kyle pulled away and nudged me towards a bean chair. I sat on it and watched as Kyle pulled another one next to me and sat on it. "I'm sorry Ash. I don't think you were ready to hear that."

"Kyle, you knew. Why didn't you tell me?"

He shook his head and looked away. "You weren't ready and you still aren't, and anyways, you had to hear it from your brother, not from me."

"Why did he decide to tell me now? How is this even possible? Why would he ruin such an amazing night?" I asked. I didn't know what I was thinking or feeling anymore.

"Guilt makes people act beyond comprehension." Kyle said.

I sucked in a shaky breath. It felt as though there was a huge weight on my chest. I thought I had found a family. I thought I finally belonged somewhere. But Nate was the cause of my seventeen years of wondering; wondering why my parents had abandoned me, why I hadn't been precious enough to keep. It was his fault. I could have had a loving family; a dad who taught me to be tough, a mom who spoiled me and gave me advice, and a brother who protected me.

I thought back to when I had hugged Andrew goodbye. At that time, I had felt abandoned by the one person in the world whom I loved. Andrew's love for me seemed like a sham now, and it was clear Nate had never been there for me. Not once. I had no parents, nobody who truly cared for me. I felt more than abandoned; I felt alone. Abandoned and alone.

NINETEEN

I jerked out of my seat when I heard a sound outside. Since Kyle and I hadn't been talking, the sudden sound surprised me. It was probably an owl or something. Sighing, I leaned back into the beanbag and glanced at Kyle. His eyes were closed and he was snoring lightly. Seriously? While I was drowning in self pity he was sleeping? Boys will be boys.

I closed me eyes for a brief moment, wishing that I could also fall asleep, but I knew that wasn't going to happen. There were too many things going through my head. There was too much pain to deal with. I felt so betrayed. I felt so mad. And for some reason, I also felt guilty.

I was mad at Nate, but I hadn't had the right to run away like that. I probably should have stayed, walked back to the fire. I knew that he was probably drowning in guilt. But that didn't change the fact that I felt so let down and alone because of him.

All the pieces finally clicked together; the reason that I had been put up for adoption, the reason I had been adopted by a family who didn't care about me at all. I understood why Joshua and Kyle had been so secretive about taking me to their house, why they couldn't have just walked up and talked to me; they couldn't be seen. The reason that Nate and Anne had adopted Dylan and Maya; he felt he needed to adopt them so that he would feel less guilty about leaving me, but I also knew that Nate loved Dylan and Maya like his own children.

I understood why no one knew and—why no one could know—

where Nate lived. I understood why the kids didn't go to school.

Everyone would ask them questions and eventually find out that Nate was their father —parent-teacher meetings, graduation, science fairs, etc...— and people finding out would stir trouble.

I also wondered. What happened after the house burned? Did anyone find out it was partly Nate's fault? Would he have been arrested for buying drugs? With a sigh, I realized that I would have to ask him soon. I couldn't hide in the shadows forever. I would eventually need to know what had happened. But not now. Now I just needed to forget what had happened. I needed fresh air.

I climbed out of the secret area and stepped onto the forest floor, crunching some leaves in the process. I closed my eyes and inhaled...smoke?

Quickly opening my eyes, I shut them again. I was imagining things. Why else would I be seeing a yellowish orange-ish light in the dark? I opened my eyes. Nope, it was definitely there. It took me a moment to realize what it was, but when I did, I let out a scream. Before I could blink, Kyle was at my side, looking at me with concern. When he saw that I was staring straight ahead he moved his gaze to what I was staring at and sucked in a sharp breath.

This had to be a joke. This had to be a dream. Why else would I be seeing fire?

"No. This can't be happening. Where is everybody?" Kyle yelled.

As if on cue we saw a figure running towards us. That figure turned out to be Leah.

When she reached us, she doubled over, breathing heavily.

"What happened?" Kyle demanded.

"They all left" —she panted, sucked in air— "I had to guard the" —pant, breath— "the fire" —pant, breath— "then there was this sound, and I don't know what happened!" she said, tears streaming down her cheeks.

"Leah, calm down and tell us exactly what happened."

She coughed, leaned on her knees and took a few deep breaths. When she stood up she looked a bit calmer.

"Okay, so when you ran off, Nate told us that you left. He said that we had to split up to try to find you. Everyone left and I was supposed to stay by the fire in case you came back. Then I sort of fell asleep." She sucked in a breath. "Then I heard this weird sound. I don't know what it was. A scream or something, and I woke up and there was smoke everywhere and the" —her breath hitched— "the fire was burning trees around me, and" —she choked on her words and started crying again— "and I don't know how it happened. Everything was fine and then the fire was everywhere and the smoke was everywhere and I couldn't breathe and I couldn't think, I just ran, and it's all my fault!" A sob escaped her and she put her hand over her mouth.

I went over to her and hugged her tightly. This wasn't her fault. It was mine. I should never have run off.

"Okay, no time for crying," Kyle said. "We need to find the others. Follow me!" He started running, and Leah and I followed.

"Kids! Where are you? Kids!" We heard a voice yelling somewhere to the right.

Following the voice Rana, Mark, Anne, Josh, and Nate soon

came into view. They didn't even ask what had happened, they just pulled us in for a hug, but only for the tiniest second.

"Dad, I'm so sorry, I really didn't mean to, I don't know what happened—" Leah started.

"Don't worry about that now. We'll talk about it later. Now we need to find Cynthia, Dylan, and Maya."

That's when I realized that they weren't with us. I started to panic. "Um Nate, where did you ask them to go?" I asked, not looking him in the eye.

"I told them to check the house." There was panic in his voice. "I'm going to go find them!" he said.

As he spoke, I noticed a few figures running towards us. Thank God! They were safe. They neared us and I felt a sense of relief wash over me. But before I could truly relax, I saw the horror on their faces. Nate froze mid run and stared at them.

"Maya's still in the house!" Dylan yelled. "We couldn't get to her!"

No. Please no. This couldn't be happening.

Nate started running again, but Dylan stopped him. "Dad! We were there. There's no way to get her out. You need to call an ambulance and fire fighters. Come on! There's no time to waste!"

Josh pulled out his phone and started dialing a number. He was talking, but I couldn't hear him. Dread washed over me. Maya had to be alright. If something happened to her, I didn't know what I would do. This could not be happening.

Soon sirens blared in the distance and neared us, there was water, people shouting and running. It felt far away. My limbs felt numb and I didn't recall breathing but I must have been. Then I started coughing and the world came back into focus. Smoke. For some reason I had not noticed the smoke till that moment. I couldn't get in enough oxygen and every breath in turned into a cough. Suddenly, the world was spinning and everything went black.

TWENTY

Where was I? I heard a steady rumbling. Something rubbery pushed against my cheek and the growling noise defined itself as the purr of an engine. I was momentarily jolted up and down. I was in a car. Opening my eyes, I squinted at the red lights flashing on and off. An ambulance.

The rubber turned out to be a mask on my face. I yanked it off and sat upright. Three men in white doctors' coats stood around me. One was trying to talk to me, but I wasn't listening. I moved from side to side, looking for a familiar face, the feeling of panic building in me again.

"Maya! Where's Maya?" My voice was hoarse and raspy. I coughed a few times.

"Honey, you need to calm down," someone was saying.

"Maya! Where's Maya! Maya! Where are you? Where is she?" Something pierced my skin, there was a burning in my veins and then my eyes closed again.

A beeping woke me up. I found myself in a strange room with white walls and cold features. I was on a bed with a tube in my arm. White sheets. I saw and felt their texture on my fingers; stiff with bleach. A medium-sized TV blared with cartoons on a white stand. A hospital room, my mind said. How had I gotten here?

A nurse walked into the room, and as her heels clicked on the tiles my mind started whirring, recalling the events of the night before.

"Where's my family? Where is everyone?" I sat upright and started pulling at the pipes taped to my arms.

"Oh good, you're awake. Don't worry about your family for now," she said and gently removed my hand from my own wrist. I really wanted to punch something.

"Where. Is. My. Family?" I asked again.

The nurse sighed. "There were three others who fainted from all the smoke but they're fine now."

"Maya. Maya, is she fine?" I asked urgently. The nurse sighed and grabbed her clipboard. She walked out of the room without answering my question and I fumed at her tap-tapping as she disappeared down the corridor. How rude!

I laid back and let out an angry breath. The door creaked and I bolted up, ready to demand answers from the nurse. But it wasn't the nurse, it was Nate.

"Nate, thank God! What happened to Maya? Is she okay? Where is she? How are the others?" I couldn't help the thudding of my heat and my palms felt clammy. I squeezed them against the sheets and bit my lip.

"Maya isn't okay. They found her unconscious. We haven't heard about her since." A tear streaked from his eye to his jaw. "Anne took a few tests to see if the baby was fine, and thank God, there are no problems regarding her pregnancy. Leah, Dylan, and Cynthia also collapsed after having inhaled too much smoke. But they have all woken up and they're fine. Dylan and Cynthia have already been allowed out of their hospital rooms and will be discharged a bit later today. You and Leah will be allowed to come out soon too, after a few tests confirming you're back to your old selves." He sat on the edge of my bed and patted my foot, but he wouldn't meet my eyes.

"Look, I know this is probably not the time, but I wanted to tell you Ash, I'm really, really sorry. I was eighteen and stupid." The quiet felt choking. "Ash, please forgive me."

I was going to cry again, I could feel it. "Let's not talk about it. I was really inconsiderate to run off like that. I just felt so betrayed and alone, you know? I needed time to myself. But the past is the past. You can't do anything about it. Besides, we have other things to worry about."

"Thanks Ash." Still not looking at me, he stood and walked to the door, pausing as if he might say something, then shaking his head instead. He closed the door with a click of finality.

Two hours later I was out of the hospital room and in the waiting room, waiting for news about Maya. Everyone was here – except Maya, obviously. We were all waiting in anticipation. No one spoke. No one really had to. There was nothing to say. Kyle tapped a finger against a coffee cup. Nate and Anne held hands tight, her head leaning against his shoulder, she frowned with closed eyes.

The twins sat silently and stared out a window, and the others had their eyes trained on the floor. I hoped Maya was okay. If she wasn't, it would be my fault. If I hadn't run off, no one would have left to search for me and the fire wouldn't have somehow caught onto a tree. It was my fault. Right then and there, I realized I knew just how Nate felt. He must have felt as guilty as me. Probably more so. Now I understood. And I knew that I had forgiven Nate.

A doctor walked into the room.

"Mr. and Mrs. Coffman?" he asked and all of us stood and rushed towards him. He took a step back.

"You're all family?" he asked, clutching his clipboard close to his chest and eyeballing the twins.

"Yes. Is there news about Maya?" Anne asked.

The doctor looked down at his clipboard and sighed.

"I'm sorry," he said with sadness. Oh no. This couldn't be good. "She's not going to make it..." That's all I heard, nothing more. I sank to my knees on the floor. This couldn't be happening. I felt tears streaming down my face, and I heard someone yelling. We were all a mess.

This couldn't be happening. I put my hands over my face. This couldn't be happening. My heart rate had gone up. This couldn't be happening! First I lost my parents to a fire, and now I was going to lose my best friend. This couldn't be happening.

"Ashley, you can go in now," I heard someone tell me and I stood stonily from my seat. We were all taking turns saying our last words to Maya. There was a possibility that she could hear us, but the doctors couldn't be sure. All the doctors knew was that she only had a few hours to live. That's all they knew.

I walked to the door and shakily opened it. I gasped when I saw the state that Maya was in. She was burned all over and she had a mask on her face and several tubes attached to her. This was my fault. I let out a breath and sat down on a chair next to Maya. I needed to be strong. These were going to be my last words to her, and I needed to be strong. I held Maya's hand and I started talking to her.

"I never had a real friend. I never had anyone who truly understood me; someone who I could count on. Someone to share secrets with. Someone to go on adventures with. I was never shy, I just didn't talk to people. I guess I just expected people to talk to me. They never did –until you."

I let out a sob and bent my head as tears started to stream down my face. Maya's hand was cold in mine and I squeezed it, wanting to bring some warmth.

"You were bubbly and happy and by just looking at you, I knew that you were the type of girl that makes a difference; the type of girl that changed the world. I always admired you, Maya. Always have, always will. You are so brave to have endured all that you endured. I would have broken already if I were you." My hair was sticking to my face because of all the tears and my heart was hurting.

"You made me understand what it was like to have a shoulder to lean on. People like you are rare, and I'm so lucky to have you. So, so lucky. I know I never told you this, so I'll tell you now. You're my best friend, Maya, and I love you."

As I looked down at Maya's burnt face I felt as if I would never smile again; as if life would lose all of its colors once she was gone. No amount of tears would suffice to express the amount of sadness that I wanted to radiate. She was my first real friend.

I stared at her as tears flowed down from my cheeks, as my stomach wrenched and my heart ached and then, I let go of her hand and I let her go.

TWENTY-ONE

6 months later...

We were all in the waiting room of a hospital, waiting in anticipation. But this time, for a completely different reason. Anne was giving birth! It was the fourth of January and I had been sleeping when Josh barged into my room to let me know that we were going to the hospital. I looked around at everyone and I felt a smile come to my face. So much had changed in the past six months.

After Maya had passed away, we had all been heart-broken, but we knew she would have wanted us to be strong for her, so we all tried to be. I thought of her everyday, and I'm pretty sure everyone else did too. There were times when one of us would break down and start crying, but the thing was, we all had each others' back.

I still felt guilty for what had happened. I still felt like it was all my fault, but I knew that guilt would not turn back the clock. Guilt wouldn't do anything. I completely understood how Nate felt, and I forgiven him.

It was still a mystery how the fire had caught onto a tree, and it was probably just bad luck.

I went to talk to my adoptive parents, to Andrew, to my aunt and uncle, and finally, to Sara. I had sorted everything out, I explained everything from beginning to end, and Nate met my adoptive family, although he already knew them because he had been paying them to take care of me. Luckily Sara turned out to be okay, and she couldn't remember what had happened to her, which was great. Nobody knew I had knocked her unconscious because of the locket, and it was just as well.

Nate and Anne had bought a new house, in a nice neighborhood, out of the hiding. There had been a fundraising event for them and they had enough money for a cozy and homey house and for all the furniture they needed.

I had turned eighteen a few months ago, and since I was a legal adult, I could live wherever I wanted to. Nate and Anne told me that I could stay with them, and I gratefully accepted. I wasn't sure where and when I wanted to go to university.

The fire incident brought the whole family closer together, and through the good and bad, we helped each other, lifted each other up. Although Kyle didn't talk much, I had gotten really close to him in the past few months. It turned out that we liked doing the same types of things; football, swimming, and video games.

My locket was still around my neck; I never took it off. But now, instead of just the picture of my parents on one side, there was also a picture of Maya on the other.

"Guys, do you want to see your new sister?" Nate asked, snapping me out of my thoughts. "And in Ash's case, niece."

We stood up at the same time and shoved our way towards the hospital room where Anne was, each eager to be first to lay eyes on the new baby. "Oh my goodness, she's so cute!"

"What's her name?"

"I hope she doesn't cry!"

"I call dibs on never having to change her diaper."

"She's so pretty!"

"Can we exchange her for a boy?"

Everyone was talking at once and I tried to push through them so that I could see my niece.

Then I saw her. Her eyes were closed and her chest was moving up and down as she breathed steadily. Her little hand was curled around Anne's finger, and she was wrapped in a pink blanket. I went towards the baby girl and gasped when she suddenly opened her eyes. Her eyes were blue and wide open.

Then, she looked at me. I slowly held out my hand and she gripped it with her tiny fingers. Someone was asking to hold her, but I wasn't paying attention to who it was, I was so mesmerized by the little baby.

I looked away for a little while and I saw Rana standing in the corner and pouting. I slowly took my hand away from the baby and walked towards Rana.

"Hey Rana, what's wrong?" I asked.

"Evewyone loves her. They awn't goiwin' to pay attenthion to me anymowe."

"What? That's not true! Imagine how cool it will be to have a little sister! Finally you'll be able to blame everything on someone else! Also, she's going to look up to you and admire you, and try to do things like you! Won't that be cool?" I said taking her shoulder and turning her to face me.

"Maybe," she said and shrugged, and then I took her hand and led her to the baby girl. I let go, and Rana started hesitantly talking to the baby.

"My nawme iws Wana. Yow my wittle sister. I'm gowin to bwame evewything on you now." She said with a small smile.

Nate cleared his throat and everyone looked at him.

"So, we want to tell you guys what we decided to name her...." The excitement was clear on his face. "Her name is Nadia." he finished, and I froze.

Nadia, my middle name. The name I was given after I was born. They were naming my niece after me! I felt tears in my eyes, but I wouldn't let them fall; this was not a time for tears.

"Nadia, meaning hope." Nate said.

Hope. There was hope. I had learned that over time. When everything feels hopeless, just hang on to the last shred of hope you have left, and everything will be alright. Sure, there wouldn't always be fairy tale endings, but things would still be fine.

When you feel that you're alone, when you feel that you're abandoned by someone you love, have hope, because in the end you'll realize that you aren't alone, you aren't truly abandoned.

There are other people like you who think that they're alone, but they don't realize that they aren't. Alone means that no one is there for you, that no one understands you. But those people out there that think they're alone, they know what you feel. And because of that, you aren't alone. You might not be surrounded by people who love you and support your decisions, but that doesn't make you abandoned.

If you search deep enough and think long enough, you would realize that you have never truly been and will never truly be abandoned and alone.

The End

Acknowledgements

Infinite thanks to Joy for editing and improving my work. You're awesome.

Thanks to Amanda for reading everything and telling me what to change and improve. I will forever be grateful that you took interest in my writing and gave your all to help me.

Huge thanks to Pheobe Stone for creating the awesome cover and to Kari Nichols for helping me with the formatting. Thank you so, so much for all the encouragement and guidance. You're the best.

Thank you to my parents and siblings for encouraging me and believing in me from the start. I love you.
And finally, thank you Kelsie and Maria for all the motivation and love you both showed to me. You're incredible.

About the Author

Debora is a young writer who aspires to improve her own skills and inspire others. She is half Lebanese and half French and currently living in Lebanon. She loves to convey hope in her writing and everyday life, and her greatest wish is to make a difference.

CPSIA information can be obtained
at www.ICGtesting.com
Printed in the USA
LVHW111105210719
624768LV00001B/256/P